Wires and Wings

D1738678

The Puzzle Box
Chronicles: Book 4

Wires and Wings

Shawn P. McCarthy

The Puzzle Box Chronicles
Book 4

Dark Spark Press

Book cover design by Teodora Chinde
Printed in the United States of America
First Printing, 2017
ISBN-13: 978-0-9968967-6-4 (Dark Spark Press)
ISBN-10: 0-9968967-6-7

Dark Spark Press

www.DarkSparkPress.com

Publisher.DarkSparkPress@gmail.com

For

My Father

John E. McCarthy

Chapter 1

Special Interests

Footsteps echo through a dark hallway.

The sound stops suddenly. The echo does not.

The corridor, all cement blocks and tile floor, keeps the sound resonating for a few seconds after Amanda Malcom halts in front of an open door.

Squint of an eye. Turn of a head. She walks in and delivers an angry message across a desktop in no uncertain terms.

It's been five days since her good friend Jeb Thomas was locked up. Amanda has grown tired of the games. Tired of the lying. If this man, this so-called labor lawyer, is capable of helping Jeb, then he'd better do so now.

"Otherwise," she tells him, "it appears to other union men that you are not really handling the legal affairs of the union workers at all." You are just taking a fee and paying us lip service."

"I'm afraid you don't understand," the bearded attorney tells her. "There are many political winds in this town. Many things for a man like me to consider before becoming involved. You have to be patient."

"I've been very patient," Amanda replies.

The attorney's name is Nester Ryan. His office occupies the south side of the first floor in his expensive and tasteful Gothic mansion. It's a looming house that sits just off Broadway Avenue, a stone's throw from the Missouri River and the Hannibal Bridge.

Ryan is a portly gentleman, a happy victim of the general largess that slowly settles upon those who reign supreme in deskbound careers. The thick steaks. The fine wines. The after-dinner cigars. They all add up. In his case, most of it has added up around his waist and chin.

"So I suggest you consider this," Amanda says sternly. "I know the names of the highest-level union managers in this town. And I know roughly what they pay you each year to handle their affairs. I have no problem telling them about your lack of support for Jeb even as you take their money."

Ryan smiles. "Ah yes. I know full well that your concern is for Mr. Thomas. Unfortunately, it's more complicated than you seem to realize." He speaks in carefully measured tones. "This friend of yours, this Jeb, is not technically a member of the union I represent. In fact, he doesn't belong to any union in this town. Thus, I have no particular obligation to him. He is an acquaintance of the union at best, but not someone on whom we can spend a great deal of time and effort."

"And you have spent just how much time and effort on him to date?"

"I have made some inquiries on his behalf."

"And what is the status of those inquiries?"

"I'm afraid that falls under attorney-client privilege."

Amanda stands and leans over the desk, looking him in the eyes. "I would find that much more believable, Mr. Ryan, if you had actually visited Mr. Thomas. But to date, I know you have not. So it would seem that he doesn't have much of a privilege at all in your eyes."

The attorney shrugs.

"He would like you to visit and talk with him. You will be paid for your time."

"By whom?"

"Friends."

The attorney laughs. "Simple as that must seem, I again remind you that this is a more complex issue than you realize. Labor negotiations unfold slowly, I'm afraid. They always do. And such negotiations can be derailed by many things."

Amanda grits her teeth. "Such as?"

"Money, my dear. You referred to me as a labor lawyer. I suppose that's accurate since union business has become the mainstay of my practice in recent years. But, as I intimated, there's more than one union in this town. Do you understand that? Problems such as the ones raised by the appearance and subsequent arrest of your friend," he raises an eyebrow, "if I may call him your *friend*, are not simply black-and-white matters. The problem for me does not come down to whether he is union or non-union. When one union grows strong, others lose ground. Do you understand? The playing fields shift back and forth. And that's not a good thing if you are on the wrong side. Does this make sense?"

Amanda listens, nodding slightly.

"And I represent the interests of the union—"

"Which union, Mr. Ryan? Whichever one you can play off the other, keeping your business going forever?"

He scowls. "I think this conversation is over."

"For now, perhaps." She picks up her hat and slowly starts to walk toward the door. Then she turns back, looking down on him. "Do you know a Mr. Jay Gould?"

"Gould? The owner of the Missouri Pacific Railway? Yes, I do," the attorney nods.

"Mr. Gould once said, 'I can hire one half of the working class to kill the other half.' Jeb told me that. I didn't really understand it at the time, but I think I do now."

Ryan avoids her steely gaze.

"The next time we talk, I expect it will be because you intend to help a man who is a good friend and associate of your best customer, the National Progressive Union. If your other clients, the other unions, are getting in the way of that, I think the NPU might be very interested in knowing about the problem your multiple affiliations have caused, don't you?"

"You tread on thin ice, my dear."

"Perhaps I do. But how do you intend to retaliate, Mr. Ryan? Have me attacked and beaten too? Just like someone did to Jeb? Is beating a woman the sort of front-page news that will serve your cause well?"

She smiles politely and sees herself to the door, but not without feeling Ryan's icy stare on the back of her neck.

Chapter 2

Half-Full

Back in Boston, Victor Marius walks slowly away from the train station. Head hung low, he's unsure exactly where he's going or why.

He didn't sleep at all on the train ride from New York. All he knows is that he's now back home. After his bewildering visit to New York, it seemed as good a destination as any.

In the distance, he hears another train coming up the track. He doesn't turn to look. To Victor, it makes scant difference who is arriving and departing. He feels detached from the real world.

He had hoped that Tesla might have some sort of job for him in New York. But that was not to be. He had spent far too much money making the trip, and now he didn't even have enough to stay at the rooming house.

And in the middle of it all, he grew angry and threw someone off the train and into a river. It was an overreaction to a minor incident and it deeply surprised him when he did it. When it was happening, he felt on top of the world. Strong. Invincible. But the feeling waned, along with the drugs in his system.

Instinctively, he runs his hand along the length of his other arm. A few weeks ago, he was rail-thin and weak. Now, thanks to Dr. David Burke's wonder drugs, good food and a solid regimen of weightlifting and other exercises, he feels the bulkiness and sense of strength far beyond anything he's ever felt.

And now the reality of his situation has settled down on him like a shroud. Since he's returned from sea, he's spent his time recovering from his injuries but he's also wasted too much effort building his electric bicycle and experimenting with injections of steroid alcohol and other components that have helped build his muscles, but which seem to be sucking away his humanity.

"So where does this all leave me?" he asks aloud. A man passing by on the sidewalk stares back at him indifferently.

Victor feels like he's walking through a watercolor painting of some sort of zoo, looking through windows at a collection of animals he's never seen before. Nothing seems recognizable in his new world, and he doesn't like the feeling. But he can't shake it.

Victor's main reason for returning to Boston, other than having a personal history here, is that he may finally have some semblance of a job now.

Before leaving New York City, he contacted the Boston Western Union office and was told a telegram had arrived. He convinced the reluctant attendant to relay the message. It was a vague statement from the lead supervisor of a local electric company. Victor had talked to the man about three weeks earlier.

The telegram asked if he was interested in supervising a group of laborers—men who had been hired to install electric lines near the center of the city. The work, if it became available, might eventually take him to other parts of the state too. It was an open-ended offer, but it was hedged in maybes. The work, if it did materialize, could last more than a year.

The offer only makes Victor's cloudy detachment seem worse. This job isn't at all focused on research into electricity or radio waves. It's just pulling and connecting wires.

He mulls the job over in his mind. The lab is where he wants to make his living. The rote mechanics of field installations are just a distraction. It's like telling an artist to put down his brushes and do nothing but hang other people's paintings.

"Newspaper, mister?"

Victor shakes off his daydream and presses a dime into the newsboy's hand and takes the folded broadsheet. The front page of the *Boston Traveler* mentions something about construction of a new immigration facility in New York City, to be located on some speck of land called Ellis Island. With a snort, Victor flips to the next page, then to the next one, slowly reading his way down the street.

With barely enough money to eat, Victor finds himself wandering toward the North End as he finishes the last of the paper. The place where he's been staying, the rooming house, is cheap, but he needs someplace even cheaper until he gets back on his feet. On a hunch, he heads directly toward the Mariner's House. Even though he's never been inside, he knows the place well, thanks to friends of his father.

It's about 9:00 a.m. when he reaches the tall green front door of 11 North Square. He studies the spider web of small window panes, then takes a deep breath. Despite all his months at sea, he can't claim that he's worked as a sailor. He is a galoot at best—someone who is transported by a ship, but who lacks any official sea duties.

He doubts the house, which is dedicated to sailors, will consider him kin to the sailing man. But if they don't take him, perhaps the attendants can recommend some other affordable place nearby.

He yanks at the knob and walks in.

A woman with gray hair tucked up in a neat bun sits at a small table. She sips a cup of tea as she writes in a small ledger. Old paintings of sailing ships dot the walls along with some newer images of steamers. He sees a set of shelves, stuffed tight with many types of books, at the far end of the room. On the other wall is a pegboard holding an assortment of keys. If the number of keys still hanging on the board hints at the number of rooms available, it could be that the house has many vacancies. Good news for him.

"May I help you?" the woman asks, setting down her tea.

"Um, yes, I um …." Victor decides to just lay his cards on the table. "I should start by saying this. I'm not really a working sailor. I've spent many months at sea. Even survived a shipwreck. But I was always on board for other reasons. I've always been mainly a traveler or a scientist.

Shipping some equipment. Doing some engineering tests. That sort of thing."

He looks around the room, then back at her. "What I mean is, I'm not sure that I qualify to stay here. You take sailors here. I know that. I guess I was just wondering if you could recommend another affordable rooming house in this area."

She nods, then looks over at the key rack. "Well, you're correct, usually this home is only for sailors. It's their safe haven. Their support system."

She looks him up and down. She's seen his type before. Thin but beefy in the shoulders. Meager belongings held in a worn pack. Sweaty. Probably walked here rather than taking a cab.

"What sort of engineering? On what sort of ships?"

"Electrical stuff. Mostly on cargo ships."

She doesn't seem certain what electric stuff has to do with ships. "Union card of any sort?"

"No, ma'am."

"Did you ever help out in the engine room or the wheelhouse?"

"Actually yes, on a couple trips."

"Licensed for that?"

"Umm ... no."

She thinks for a moment. "Thinking of getting such a license? Or working toward it maybe?" She smiles and arches an eyebrow.

He sees where she's going, so he laughs and says, "Oh. Yes. Of course. Might get my license in a few months. Who knows?"

"Well, you're lucky. We're only half-full at the moment. Not too many ships in port. I normally wouldn't do this, but if you say you're working on getting an engineer's license, and if you have some trips under your belt already, I'd say we can call you enough of a sailor to let you stay here for a while."

"I do appreciate that, ma'am. Thank you."

She chuckles. "Oh, don't thank me too much. We need the tenants. The rules always relax a little if we need to keep our rooms full."

They talk price. He doesn't mention that he has exercise gear, including his barbell set made out of old brass weights. He figures he can slip those in sometime in the future.

The cheapest rooms, of course, are shared. There's a bunkhouse-style room on the back of the first floor. He hesitates, thinking he'd rather have a private room where he could set up a small lab table. But then he thinks of the cost and also of the social isolation.

"The big bunk room will be fine," he says. "Where can I put my things?"

Chapter 3

Muddy River

Worn streetcar wheels emit a high-pitched squeal. The sound, shrill and brutal, cuts through the morning air as passersby wince and cover their ears. The sound fades and a rattling mass of steel and wood slows to a crawl near Boston's Park Square.

As the trolley halts, people inside move toward the doors. A slight buzz can be heard a few feet above the car. That's where a pole from the roof intersects an overhead wire. Two years ago, this was the first Boston street car line to be electrified. Now several electric trolleys roam the city, and some people predict that the days of Boston's horse-drawn streetcars are numbered.

Devlin Richards stands beneath the green awning of a smoke shop, waiting for the crowd to disembark. He notices the front of the car still has its welded horse hitch in place. This trolley obviously is an older model, retrofitted to carry its electric motor. Newer cars look similar, but they come with the electric motor already in place. The horse hitch is no longer needed.

Progress.

After the other passengers exit, a dozen other people climb on board. Devlin follows, making his way to a seat near the front of the car. The trolley starts to roll again and heads north for a block, turns west on Boylston Street and begins its slow five-mile trip back toward the car barn at the Alston Railroad Depot.

Devlin has carefully chosen this car, and this trolley line. It follows a long looping route that passes through one of the busiest sections of the city. There are plenty of paying passengers who all push their coins into the change slot. He specifically noticed a few days ago that this car doesn't take tokens. The driver also carries a good supply of change.

Devlin has pulled several jobs since arriving from South Carolina several weeks ago. But until he saw this car, he never once thought about trying to rob a streetcar. It seemed risky. Even silly. Then he saw how much money they take in, and how unprotected they are, and he started to form a plan.

This is a late morning run, so by the time the car reaches the outskirts of the Back Bay Fens, Devlin knows it will carry only a few passengers. Based on other rides he took, it's likely that the coin box has not been emptied since five in the morning.

The crowd does indeed dwindle along the way, and by the time the car turns onto The Fenway, a new road that's still under construction, only one passenger remains. That person disembarks at the next station, and Devlin rides alone, with just the driver. He stands and slowly walks to the front of the car. The driver barely notices him. He's pulling at the brake handle as the tracks dip down toward Muddy River, a wide creek that runs through the heart of the serpentine park known as The Fens. But when Devlin places his hand on the toll box, the driver spins around.

"Hands off that. Company policy."

"That so?" He smiles. Are you saying that maybe I should take your change bag instead?" The driver looks up at him. Devlin smiles and nods, then starts to grab at the bag that sits beside the seat. But the driver has no intention of letting it go. He spins fast and slaps Devlin's arm. The Southerner responds with a round-house punch, knocking the driver off his perch. In the process, the man lets go of the brake handle. As Devlin reaches to retrieve the bag, the trolley starts gaining speed.

The driver groans and rolls over, trying to pull himself upright by the edge of the driver's seat. Devlin tucks the change bag into his coat and kicks the toll box several times, eventually loosening the metal container from its post. Just as it comes loose, the driver does manage to pull himself upright. He sneers at Devlin. Rather than move toward the brake lever, he tells Devlin to go to hell and prepares to jump from the car. But before he leaps, he reaches over to the dash, slaps a lever forward, then hops off just as the car accelerates downhill. The quick movement tosses Devlin backwards, away from the dash controls. He looks at the front of the car and realizes that the driver must have hit the accelerator out of spite before jumping. Devlin has no idea how to work this newfangled electric motor. If it was a horse, he could easily slow it down using the reigns.

But not this car.

Crawling forward, he grabs the accelerator handle and pushes it hard. But with a sinking heart, he realizes he's forced in the wrong direction, and now it's bent and stripped. The acceleration continues. He tries the brake handle, but the friction does little to slow the car. It can't fight the force of a jammed accelerator and a trolley that is heading down a hill.

"Fuck electricity!" He shouts in anger. "Who needs it!"

Heavy box tucked under his arm, Devlin manages to steady himself and moves toward an open area of the car, ready to make his own leap. But then he hears something. It's a small whimper coming from the back of the trolley. He spins around and sees that he's not alone after all.

In the last seat, so short that he can hardly see her, sits an elderly woman, barely able to see over the tall seat. Devlin looks at the woman, then at the front of the racing car, then back again. He's tempted to just make his leap, but hesitates.

"I don't know how to stop it!" he calls to her.

Her only response is a "no," and a whimpering "please." She looks like she's ready to cry.

He shakes his head. "God damn it."

Devlin stumbles toward the back of the car just as the trolley nears a curve. It's going much too fast. On the far side of the curve is the water of the Muddy River. Here in the middle of The Fens there are no people in sight. If the car crashes into the water, this woman is not likely to survive. Devlin might not either, so he knows the time to jump is now.

But he makes a decision that he hopes he won't regret. He'll try to take the woman with him if he can. Since he dares not drop his bag and cash box, he just grabs the woman by the back of her collar. He curses at her and pulls her into the aisle. The slats of the old wood floor rumble and bounce.

The terrible high-pitched squeal returns. This time it's not from the brakes. The sound comes from the pressure of the wheels entering the tight curve. He knows the car will eventually derail and probably flip toward the outside of the curve – toward the water, so he drags the woman and the cash box toward the other side of the trolley. Dropping to his knees, he pulls the screaming woman toward the edge and lets her tumble over. Her terrified face looks toward the sky. He keeps a tight hold on her collar, letting the woman's feet drag along the pavement. The screams continue.

"Shut up, damn you! I'm trying to save you."

With a bit of a heave, he pushes her away. She skids, rather than tumbles, along the road. As she slides to a stop, Devlin can see that she will be okay, albeit with a nice bit of road rash on her bottom.

He stands and gets ready to jump. But he suddenly feels a strange lifting sensation. The wheels on one side are lifting. The car starts to tip over. Sparks fly from the overhead wires as the rod at the top of the car pulls loose.

Devlin steps out onto the trolley's sideboard, then quickly spins around, facing the car. One hand grips his cash box. The other holds tight to a handrail. He's on the far side of the car, away from the water, and as the big square coach completes its tip toward the Muddy River, Devlin feels himself pushed higher, then launched up and over as the car completes its fall. He feels like one of the Chinese circus acrobats he saw as a child.

Holding tight to the cashbox, he pushes off with his foot at the last second, giving himself just enough height to clear the trolley as the old car spins and drops into the water.

The coach splits into multiple pieces as it impacts the water. It's mostly sections of wood and glass that break free, skipping across the water like a dozen flat stones. Devlin lands about 10 feet past the coach, coming down in an awkward splash. The landing makes him drop the cash box.

What's left of the trolley car bobs forlornly in the water.

He comes up to the surface fighting for breath and then he does a quick self-assessment. He realizes immediately that the damage to his own body is minimal, thanks to the cushioning effect of the water. But he's wearing too many clothes.

After a few puffs, he grasps the change bag and wriggles out of his coat. He treads water. This is indeed a muddy river, though it's not a terribly big one. He can't see the bottom, but it doesn't seem deep. He tosses the bag onto the bank then dives, searching, multiple times. Eventually he finds his cash box settled onto the gravel bottom of the river. Six feet deep.

It weighs enough that he can't quite swim with it to the surface. But after a few tries, he finds that he can hold it at thigh level and take a few steps along the bottom.

He bobs up for breath—one, two, three times—returning to the cash box after each breath. He is able to walk it along the bottom a few feet each time. Eventually he makes it to the shallower part of the river, and he drags his prize onto the rocks.

No one has come yet to check on the wrecked trolley. It looks like they were just out of sight – enough so that no one saw the crash. But it's highly likely the trolley driver has sent out some kind of alert. Or maybe people found that injured woman. Chances are that someone is already following the tracks around the curve and heading toward this spot.

Devlin looks around then braces the metal box against a rock. He picks up another rock and bashes a folded metal seam several times until it bends and he can get his hand inside. He scoops out the change. Handful after handful. It's not a fortune. Maybe sixty-five dollars tops. Add that to the twenty-eight dollars from the driver's change bag and it's a somewhat reasonable score.

He tries not to think about the risk he took to get it.

Devlin stuffs all of the change into the bag, then sloshes, in his wet clothes, along the riverbank. He walks downstream until he's able to find his coat, which floated ahead of him. Far behind him, there are voices. Rescuers are calling out to the crashed trolley and looking for survivors.

But he knows he's out of sight now, and likely in the clear. Anyone who is back there will surely be focusing on the wreck itself for several minutes.

He follows the Muddy River out until it meets the Charles River. There he finds a wider bank and sunny spot. He settles onto an old log, where he will sit for a while. He needs to dry out.

Another day. Another meager score. Just enough to keep going. These Yankees, definitely, are taxing his patience.

Chapter 4

News

It takes three weeks for Jeb's case to come to trial. Amanda spends her time working in the kitchen of a small hotel. A tiny room tucked near the back staircase is part of her pay.

After taking orders and clearing tables every day, she falls into bed at night with sore feet and tired arms. When she has enough energy, she reads by candlelight. In those lonely weeks, she nearly finishes the diary of Victor Marius, scanning, in nascent wonder, page after page.

What strikes her most about what she reads is the doubt and fear Victor expresses about his own path.

Why doubt? Why fear?

Compared to her, Victor seems to have made all the right choices in life. He came from humble beginnings, yet he made something of himself. He went to college. He worked at the forefront of his industry. He was a man for whom things fell neatly into place, thanks to his own hard work.

At least things looked bright for him right up until his bitter end in that terrible storm.

That he should worry so much confuses her. She could certainly teach him a thing or two about putting doubt and fear aside while holding one's head high through it all.

At last she puts the journal aside and lies back on her bed.

What would someone think if they read a journal of my life? she wonders. Would it bore them to death? She hopes that it wouldn't. She's had some interesting twists and turns along the way. And now she's waiting for her new man to get out of jail.

So what exactly is her story? Is hers a tale of comedy or tragedy? It's certainly not a story of wealth and privilege. For some reason, the thought makes her smile as she drifts off to sleep.

A tiny room. A meek, dirty job. An uncertain future. Yet a strange sense of contentment. Maybe she'll start her own journal, just to tell her story, should anyone care.

Each morning, Amanda visits Jeb at the jail, doing what she can to brighten his spirits. She shows him news clippings about his upcoming trial and brings him cookies from the hotel kitchen. In time, the guard lets her stay longer. She always sits in a straight-backed chair just outside the cell door. She and Jeb talk about the weather, politics, and anything else they can think of, just to try to brighten the mood. Their eye contact seems to wax and wane along with the moods. The smiles are few and far between.

Not long after she arrived in Kansas City, Amanda wrote a letter to the Morgans just to let them know that she was alive. When she mailed the letter, she wasn't entirely sure why she did it. Part of her just wanted to let them know what a survivor she could be.

On the day before his trial, a reply arrives from Beverly Morgan. Tearing open the envelope, Amanda walks to the back porch of the hotel and sits down to read, feet up on the railing. Beverly's tone is formal, as always.

Dearest Amanda,

What amiable surprise it was to hear from you. We have been quite curious about your status ever since your departure. Grand to hear that you have found work and lodging in Kansas City. I don't know much about that place, but I understand that it is growing quite rapidly.

Amanda reads on, learning bits and pieces of news about the neighbors, the local kids. She mentions Jasper's latest electrical tinkering, which almost caused him to electrocute himself the week before.

Then Amanda reads something that surprises her.

I must admit, dear Amanda, that I fear my ill will caused you great hardship. For that, I truly apologize. Please blame it on the fear and uncertainty of an old woman.

It may surprise you to hear this, but we all missed you from the moment you left, myself included. In spite of the occasional tension between you and me, you brightened our home, and I still think of you when I look into the carriage house and see that dreadful noisy steam car that's still parked in there. You arrived here in a flourish of noise and sparks that this neighborhood hasn't

*seen before nor since. It's amazing how quiet and uneventful
things have become since you've gone.*

Amanda smiles. She had not expected this kind of
honest correspondence from Beverly. Obviously the tension
has now been reduced by distance. It's nice that Beverly can
recall the friendly way their acquaintance started, rather
than the awkward way it ended. The graciousness of her
letter seems genuine. Amanda feels her heart ache for
Boston. She had seemed so friendless when she was there,
yet it suddenly feels like home. She knows absolutely no one
where she is now, other than the hotel kitchen staff.

This place isn't home. She misses home.

Her eyes drop down to the final few paragraphs,
dashed off in a shaky hand that seems to have grown tired
of the pen.

*Oh, and remember that Mr. Tesla you once asked about? I
don't know who this person is exactly, but Jasper mentioned the
name and he wanted me to tell you, if I ever heard from you again,
that Jasper asked his nephew and the nephew says Mr. Tesla has
moved to New York. He thought this Mr. Tesla might be
interested in knowing about the last days of that sailor who is
mentioned in that diary you found. Apparently there are some
people, Mr. Tesla and Jasper's nephew included, who were quite
interested in what the diary writer was doing out on the water.
Must have been something important.*

Anyway, if you are interested, I can find out more, and maybe you can write him a letter someday or pay him a visit if you return back east.

That's all the news I have, dear. Again, I apologize for our difficulties. Be well, and God bless.

With fondness,

Beverly

Amanda sits for several minutes on the porch, watching a sparrow peck at the pile of bread crumbs she threw over the rail the previous evening.

So Beverly didn't hate her? The ever-stoic Beverly didn't see her as a nasty, devious threat to her home?

"Well, that's reassuring," Amanda says out loud.

Or maybe that's just what she wanted Amanda to think. The apology was ambiguous. It didn't include any sort of invitation to return. Perhaps the letter was prompted by nothing more than guilt on Beverly's part. But it was still satisfying to learn that the old lady had some second thoughts about the whole matter.

"You know," Amanda tells the sparrow, "I wrote to her half out of spite. I wanted to let her know that being nearly evicted from their home hadn't dampened my spirits. I'm still a survivor!"

The bird cocks its head, looks at her, then flies away.

Amanda knows that she also wrote to Beverly as a sort of peace offering. She felt remorseful about the trouble she had caused just by showing up at their doorstep. She wanted to let them know that, in the grand scheme of things, she had moved on, and that she appreciated whatever kindness they had been able to show her when she needed it.

What a surprise to hear that she is actually missed. She knows she could never live there again, but it makes her smile to hear that word. To hear that she had brightened their house. It feels good.

To be missed. Someplace, by some people, for some reason. Tentative as it is, it still gives her a warm feeling.

Chapter 5

Right and Proper

Things are finally looking up for Devlin Richards. He can't claim to be financially well off. Not yet anyway. But at least his meager take from the electric trolley, plus a few other jobs, has left him with a little cash that should last for a couple of weeks or more.

The idea of heading back toward his bleak room gives Devlin an empty feeling. It's a warm Saturday night. Lights still burn. Windows remain open. Laughter and shouting fill the air. So he wanders on, aimless, but still looking and listening.

Eventually he finds himself near the water. But this time it isn't the rough area by the docks. Instead, he walks through the areas where import and export businesses have their offices. This is a place where a few nice houses are tucked here and there between large warehouses and marketplaces dedicated to bulk trading.

He hears music coming from one of those fine houses and decides to walk toward the sound. He immediately realizes what the place is. There's something about the lights, and the arrangement of the curtains. Something about the people lingering outside and the type of bawdy piano rifts coming through the windows. The house is set well away from other residential districts. It's an entity unto itself, and for good reason.

Devlin closes his eyes and listens. It's an old Stephen Foster song, popular during the waning years of the war. He never understood why Foster, a Northerner, wrote so many songs about the south. But like many Southerners, Devlin has always enjoyed them.

It's good to hear this one again. The song is *Beautiful Dreamer*, but it soon slows then devolves into a different song, *Gentle Annie*. Without even thinking about it, Devlin hums along with the tune and finds himself climbing the front stoop, and stepping inside. He's still not used to these newer style houses with their large windows and bump-out sections. But the interior is quite pretty.

Most of the first floor of the large house has been opened up and converted into a sprawling parlor. Four different couches line the far wall, each with a few chairs placed in front, creating a series of inviting and semi-private sitting areas. Potted ferns and foldable Chinese screens stand between the spaces. Two of the couches are occupied with visitors. Low tables in the other two spaces hold glasses and pitchers of ice water.

Some of the crowd linger near a triangle-shaped bar in the back-left corner of the room. Bartenders wearing dark bowlers and red armbands pour whiskey and beer. Devlin can count about 30 men and roughly a dozen women. Some of the men don't seem interested in the bar, nor the couches or the women. Instead they sit at poker tables near the middle of the room.

Devlin walks over to the longest of the bar's three sides and orders a bock draft. It's slightly out of season, but they have it and it's mighty tasty. Taking a seat on one of the stools, he closes his eyes and listens to the piano.

"Good evening to you, sir. Can't say as I've seen you here before."

Devlin doesn't open his eyes. Based on the voice alone, he forms an image of the woman who is addressing him. Probably about 19 years old. Small in stature but plump around her bottom. Medium brown hair maybe? She lacks any clear accent to hint at where she is from, and the structure of her words, while disjointed, is fairly acceptable. She doesn't sound dirt poor.

He guesses, still without taking a look, that she probably ended up here through unfortunate circumstances.

Then he opens his eyes. He was close, age-wise and body-wise, but the girl's hair is darker than he imagined and her features betray something. A slight hint of mulatto. Maybe one-eighth black? Maybe even less. But it's definitely there.

"My first visit," he replies. "Didn't even know this place was here."

She climbs onto the stool next to him. "What brought you in?"

He chuckles. "The music. Just the music." He can see that his response confuses her. But she's not ready to give up on the conversation. She hesitates in her response though. Devlin just smiles and watches her youth betray her. Then he turns back to his drink.

He hasn't been to many houses like this, but he's been to enough to know that when a woman comes up to talk to a man, it starts almost like a dance. No two dancers ever are the same. Yet, by feeling the rhythm of the other, by stating one's purpose with a tip of the head or a nuance of the voice, the dance can continue. Enigmatic empathy gains dexterity with age and experience.

"So you like music?" she asks. "Would you like to dance?"

He laughs again. "Actually I was just thinking about some sort of dance. But… no. No thank you, my dear."

"So you just want to listen. All right. That's fine. Men come in here for many different reasons."

Devlin nods. "Indeed, we do. How old are you?"

"Oh, that doesn't matter, I can…"

"Nineteen? Twenty?"

"Twenty," she replies.

"I'm more than old enough to be your father."

"So are most of the men who come through that door. They mostly are the ones who can afford to be here. In fact…"

Devlin holds up a finger. "Tell you what. How about if I buy you a drink and then send you on your way, hum?" Your manager can't give you a hard time for that. You did your best. And I'm sure that bartender will overcharge me anyway."

She stands and waves him off. "Don't bother. Have a good evening."

Devlin nods, closes his eyes again, and goes back to listening to the piano. But he slowly opens them again. He looks around the room. What the girl said about the men here being at least a little wealthy looks to be true. He should be scanning the crowd for a new mark, not just sipping his beer.

He's preoccupied enough, looking over the room, that he doesn't notice another woman slide into the seat beside him. What he does feel is a wisp of breath on the back of his neck. He turns to see a much older, very elegant woman staring him in the eyes.

"Daphne is one of my best girls," she says. "I'm surprised she didn't hold your interest."

He laughs cheerfully, and realizes it's the first good laugh he's had in weeks. "Oh, believe me, she was very nice. And if I was a younger man, I might have continued to chat."

"Ahh, so you don't like them young? That certainly makes you a bit different than most of the men who come in here."

"Mmm... I don't much like poker either. Guess I fall outside of your traditional customer group."

She reaches over and straightens his collar. "I heard you tell Daphne you came in for the music?"

"I did. Yes. It reminds me of home."

She smiles at him. "Thought I heard a bit of a southern accent on you."

"Just a bit, eh?"

She holds his gaze. For a moment. Then for longer. She looks away. Then right back again. "My name is Irene. And you are…?"

He inhales. Long and slow. Thinks of a couple of fake names. But for some reason, he blurts out his real one.

She grins. "How unusual. I've never met a Devlin before. Sounds wicked."

She winks at him.

"So I've been told. But it's an old family surname. Gaelic. Great grandfather."

She lifts a finger to the bartender, who quickly refreshes Devlin's bock. He also places white wine in front of Irene. "I'm Irish myself. Somewhere along the line. And some French." She leans in a bit. That breath again. Terribly close. "Most family names come with a deeper meaning. What's yours?"

The piano plays a new tune. The red velvet curtains and the heavy Persian carpets help make everything seem muted and delightfully private.

Devlin smiles. "I was told that the very old family name was Dobhuilen, which apparently meant "Raging Valor." He stares into the foamy top beer and smirks. "I, um, I guess I got the raging part right anyway. But the name had changed to something more simple by my great grandfather's time. His name was John Devlin. Not sure if his valor was ever raging."

She places a hand on top of his. It's a subtle and sincere gesture that gives him a strange but not at all unpleasant chill. "Valor comes in many forms, you know. It also can mean determination. Or courage when the odds are stacked against you. Does that sound at all like your family?" She leans closer. "Or like you?"

He pulls his hand away, but pats hers a bit before doing so.

"I didn't come in for this."

"Oh, that's right." She sips at her wine instead. "You came for the music. And you stayed."

He nods. "And what about you? What's your last name?"

"Fitzgerald."

"Figures. Here in Boston. Should I believe you?"

"I don't care what you believe, Mr. Richards. In this house, people believe all sorts of things. It's part of our charm, no?"

He shrugs. Says nothing.

"I don't think I scare you, Devlin. I scare some men. It's funny. Even strong, tough men are scared of me sometimes. But I don't see any such fear in you. Maybe a bit of rustiness when it comes to women. And maybe an uncertainty about what it is you want, and why you haven't up and walked out of this house yet."

"I still have two-thirds of a beer to drink."

She nods and picks up her wine and holds it high. "In that case… to hidden, but not raging, valor!"

"Indeed," Devlin replies. He clinks her glass and takes a long sip.

They chat for more than 45 minutes. And against his better judgement, he does end up escorting her to her suite on the third floor. It's away from the other girls' rooms, and well away from the noise of the first-floor parlor. They came upstairs because she promised to let him have a taste of the 16-year-old scotch she keeps in her roll-top desk.

Two glasses. She pours. Then they make idle chit-chat for several minutes.

"You're very good, you know," Devlin says as he settles back into the plush divan. The fabric fits in nicely with the rest of the room, whose paintings and furniture seem to be a mix of Ottoman Empire and French Provincial.

"How so?" She brushes his hair back from his head. Tousles it. Takes a long sip from her silver glass.

"I did not come here with any intention of talking to a woman. Much less visiting her room. Yet here I am. And somehow, since about the middle of that second beer, I feel that I've somehow seduced you, not the other way around."

She nods. "Well, maybe you have more talent than you realize?"

Devlin shakes his head. "You know nothing of my talents."

She licks the scotch from her lips. "Ah. But perhaps I will?"

That wink again.

He changes the subject. "So, this is a large suite you have here. What's in the other rooms?"

She smiles. "Oh, so many things. And for now, those doors are locked. We all have our secrets, Mr. Devlin."

He raises his glass, for their second toast of the night.

"Actually," Irene says, glint in her eye, "I may know a bit about you. Secret or not. Want to hear it?"

"Do tell!" This time, it's he who holds her gaze.

"Okay. Let's start with that watch. The one you took out to look at when you felt our conversation wane just a bit down at the bar. It's gold with fancy decorations and jewels on the fob. Now, you are well bred and articulate enough, my good man, but you are not the sort of man, in your current clothes and circumstances, to own something that fine and expensive."

He shrugs. "Old family heirloom."

"Ah, but you're from the South. And that's a Waltham watch. Made right here in Massachusetts. A relatively new one too. So that tells me you likely obtained it in some other way."

He shoots her a serious look. "What other way?"

"No matter." Now, the boots. They're old and scuffed. But well-polished. You are a man used to keeping up appearances, despite circumstances. Good breeding, it seems. That's a level of training that's not gone to waste despite your current circumstances. And your love of music. You were raised in fine parlors and with people who appreciated more than just the down-home jug and fiddle bands that likely played in your area. Am I right?"

He shrugs, but he does so in a way that lets her know she hit fairly close to home.

"And now you travel. And find your money in other ways. Your hands are strong, but they lack the calluses one might see on a working man. You have several small, almost unnoticeable scars on your chin, cheeks and wrists. They are thin scars. The results of fights. Knife jabs that you managed to mostly avoid."

He looks at her.

"It very much appears that you make your living as I do, Mr. Devlin. By your wits. You break laws. You take what you can. The trouble is, you were not raised into the life the way I was. Something drove you here. But you never fully committed to it. At least, not until recently. Oh, and by the way, I know that you have a knife in your boot. I can see the bulge. Noticed it while I was looking for other bulges."

He raises his eyebrows. "You do cut right to the heart of things, don't you?"

She smiles. "My guess, good sir, is that you have less than $30 in your wallet. Now, that amount usually is more than enough for a man to come in here and have a good time. But you are sitting with the owner of this fine house. You have occupied her time for close to 90 minutes now, and you now are in her private chambers, drinking her best scotch. For most men, that is far more than they can afford."

He laughs "You're that good, hum?"

She leans in close. "Yes. I'm that good."

"So, if you think that's all the money I have in my wallet, why invite me here at all?"

She pulls back from him and plays with her hair a bit. "Maybe a few reasons. Maybe I fancy the chance to talk with someone who is educated and a bit worldly. One tires of businessmen who spend their whole days in their counting houses. Boring lads. All of them. Or maybe I just wanted to know your story. You looked out of place here." She looks directly at him now. "Or maybe, just maybe, I want a good fucking tonight. Hum? And for a change, I want it from someone who knows how to do it right and proper."

Devlin tries to smile, but it forms a bit sideways. "I… I'm flattered. But why do I feel like there's one more 'maybe' hanging in the air?"

"Well, we have a bit of a sliding scale here, you know. Part of what I charge depends on what the other person brings to the table. You've certainly kept me entertained, Mr. Devlin. I'll give you that. Think you have other services to offer me?"

"Sexual?"

"Business, silly."

He takes another drink. A gulp this time. The silver glass feels heavy in his hand. He rises, finds the bottle, and pours them both another glass. "All right. Go on."

"I have regular customers here. This is their safe haven. You won't touch them. Ever. That's rule one."

"Okay."

"But there are others. Visitors. Rivals of my friends. People who come here to outbid, outbuy and outtrade the folks that help keep me in business. Now, don't get me wrong. If they come through the door, I'm happy to make them feel welcome and take their money too. But ultimately, those visitors are bad for my long-term business. They come and go from Boston too quickly for me to establish any relationship with them. And they ultimately make the purses of my regular customers a bit thinner because of the competition they bring."

She slides closer to him. "Now those men, Mr. Devlin, have so much to offer us, and they don't even realize we're interested." She nuzzles his neck. "I've had various helpers here over the years. The men with strong hands and wounded hearts. Men who understand that it's okay to take, sometimes, for the cause." She strokes his cheek. "Our cause."

"I don't know, my dear. I tend to work alone."

Her hand slides into his lap. "I hope you realize, there are some things that you just shouldn't do alone."

It takes a few more minutes, but they eventually agree to certain terms and conditions. And much later in the evening, she confides in him that he does indeed know how to do things "right and proper."

Chapter 6

Power Punch

It's been many days since Victor invented his "wired fist." After knocking one man silly with it, he quickly put the contraption away. In his mind, he labeled it dangerous and kind of silly.

But he made the mistake of describing it to Thurman, his friend from the previous rooming house. Thurman seemed thoroughly fascinated with the idea when he first heard Victor describe the set-up. Apparently, that fascination lingered. Tonight, he stops by to see Victor. He has an idea to pitch.

Victor's friend is extremely taken with the idea that a man can attach electric wires to his hand and significantly amplify the impact of his punch. "Can you imagine making hundreds of those?" He asks Victor. "Your invention could be like the next revolver. It could be something that everyone thinks they need to protect themselves. Like a great equalizer."

Victor shakes his head. The notion, he tells Thurman, is absurd. "The shock is more of a surprise than it is deadly. "

The two lean over their beers in the backyard. The yellow reach of the low-hanging sun makes everything seem like it's made of honey. It's Victor's favorite time of the day, and he suggested that they simply sit outside to have a drink when Thurman asked if Victor wanted to go to a pub.

"Also, this rig isn't as small as you think, Thurm. Certainly not as portable as a revolver. And it takes a heavy battery. Wires can't be too long. I taped them in place over a rubber glove, but they're prone to slipping around. I mean… it just doesn't really work like you think."

Thurman laughs. "You used it, what, one time?"

"Yes."

"But it worked then, right?"

"I think I got lucky. Plus, the other guy was just kind of clueless and surprised by the shock. He mostly backed down because he hadn't experienced anything like that before."

Thurman takes a long swig and stares at the setting sun. "Okay. Hold on. Let me think. You've got something remarkable, but maybe it's not totally functional. So what do you do with it? Show it off? Look for funding to perfect it and then make a whole bunch more of them?"

"I could never get a patent. It's just a battery and wires. Anyone could make it, probably cheaper than I can."

Thurman nods. Then a bit of a grin spread over his face. "Well then, since it's designed to help you punch, why not fight with it? It worked once, right? Why not pull a John L. Sullivan move and take on all comers? You don't have to punch as hard as Sullivan does! You have a secret extra power in your fist."

"That's ridicul…" But Victor stops before he finishes his thought. He looks at Thurman, then at his beer, then he too looks at the sun. Finally, he speaks. "Okay… that's a strange but not totally preposterous idea. How would it work? How would we make money?"

Thurman tries to describe a scene for Victor. "Well, you're not going to easily attract your own crowd. No one has heard of you, and we don't have any money to advertise. But there's a ready-made crowd that goes to the Friday night fights. That's right down where we saw Sullivan punching everyone's lights out. Let's say we just set up a spot right near the gate. I'll work with you. I'll be your barker. We'll gather a crowd. Or maybe you fight me first and I take a dive. We'll make some noise. The trick will be to make you look like some sort of evil genius. People will watch then. I guarantee it!"

He chuckles. "You know, Victor, we wouldn't even need to hide what we're doing. We put it right out there. It's an electric fist! Can you survive a punch? Can you go one round with the Electric Kid? Or some nonsense like that. I *know* we could come up with a good pitch."

"Once again, how do we make money?"

"Two ways. People pay to challenge you. We promise something cheap as a prize. Just a trophy maybe. Not cash. This part is tricky because if the price is too steep, only the guys who know they're good at fighting will sign up. But if you make it just a dollar, you'll get plenty of fools. I know you can do all right in an average fight."

"So, what's the second way to make money?"

"We take bets."

Victor frowns. But he knows the idea could work. "There is a big problem though. The battery doesn't really last. I'd only be good for a few fights."

"Think you could get ten to twenty quick hits out of it?"

"I don't know. Maybe eight to ten."

"Well, that's when we change our betting strategy. We would need to involve other people. Shills. But at a certain point, after you've won a few rounds, we start betting against you as the battery drains and as you get tired."

"Sounds dangerous."

The sun slowly goes down, and they discuss various ways the plan might unfold. Victor can't do this immediately. He needs to look at a building within the next day or two as a potential place to build his new lab. But they will definitely come back to it.

One thing is for certain: it's such an outlandish idea that they know they must give it a shot.

Chapter 7

By Nightfall

On the morning of the trial, Amanda arrives at the courthouse nearly an hour early and takes a seat at the back of the main room. She's never knitted before, but she bought some supplies at a small general store, and for the past day or two she has been trying her hand at the craft. It occupies her hands as she waits. It allows her to channel nervous energy into something productive.

The trial starts late. After a few minutes, she becomes aware of conversations in the hall, and of a group of people walking the length of that hallway. They head toward the front door, whispering as they go. When she rises to look out the door, she sees the group walking away. Turning around, she sees Jeb, wounds mostly healed now, walking unescorted up the hallway. He sees her and breaks into a jog, giving her a tight embrace and a fervent kiss as they meet.

She kisses him back, realizing how much she has missed the touch of his lips and hands. "You? Walking all alone? But how? Why?"

"I'm not sure yet. I only know that Ryan, the damn labor attorney, showed up, talked to a few people and showed them some papers. The charges were suddenly dropped." Jeb kisses her again. "I wonder if you had anything to do with his decision."

"Little me?" she replies. "Why, how could someone like me ever convince a man like that to do anything?"

He laughs out loud, then adds, "By the way, the charges were dropped with one stipulation."

She pulls back, a quizzical look in her eyes.

"I have to leave here immediately."

"By when?"

"By tonight. We have to get to the railyard immediately. I need help to get out."

He holds her hand, and they walk out of the courthouse, into the first sunlight he's seen as a free man, after so many days. "Come with me," he whispers as they stand at the base of the steps.

"With you. To where? The train station?"

"Beyond that. Before they arrested me, I was planning to go to Butte, Montana. Then eventually on to San Francisco. Come with me to both. Can you?"

"What?" She pulls back even more, not sure if this invitation is good or bad.

"You heard me. I have to go to a huge copper mine in Butte. It shouldn't take us too long there. Just helping with some contract negotiations. Then to the docks on the West Coast. The work in San Francisco may be a long-term thing for me, Amanda. It may be a place to hang our hats. Maybe for good."

He smiles at her, and she tries to smile back. "I don't know, Jeb. It's so far away. And there's so much to think about between us. We're moving awfully fast."

"But where else would you go?"

She lifts her shoulders. They both know she has very few options at the moment, save staying right here and sleeping in her little cubby.

"A friend in California has written me several times to come out there, but I've never been able to make the trip. This seems like the right time. I need to put some distance between us and this place."

He takes her by the elbow and walks her toward the tall door while she wraps her excess yarn around her knitting needles.

"Jeb, Jeb, Jeb. I don't know what to say. I need to think. Let's talk about Montana first. Why go there? What's going on?"

"The Butte Mine Company. Big labor issues. Big rally coming up."

"But you mentioned a contract. What does the rally have to do with contract negotiations?"

He laughs. "That's always the way it starts. A big rally to show solidarity. Group together and make some noise. Show that we're serious and working as a team."

She shakes her head as they walk toward the station. "I don't know, Jeb. It's all so dangerous, what you do. Look what just happened to you! I don't know if I can live like this."

"But that's why San Francisco is important. That will be different."

"How so?"

"I have a bit of work to do first, but after that, I think I can land a different sort of job, Amanda. I'll still be involved in labor. I always will be. But I think I can get a job as the actual head of a local union. That's what they're asking for. I'd actually be a foreman on a dock, but I'd also be the main union representative and negotiator. No more travel. No more trouble. Work during the day and home at night for supper."

She smiles. "A normal life? For you?"

"Just as normal as it can be."

"And you want me to go with you?"

"Not just go with me. I want you to stay with me."

She hugs him. Not sure what to say, but loving the fact that he has asked.

"San Francisco is a marvelous place, Amanda," he continues. "Steep hills, view of the bay from many places. Strangely cold and foggy at times, but lovely. And the people? Friendliest place I've ever been. There are a few old families that have been there forever, but it's not like New England. You don't seem to see the same sense of old money and social status there. Everyone in town seems to have come from somewhere else, and they all seem to like it that way."

She holds his hand as they walk.

"Tell me more about this place where you'd be working."

"It's just a big pier along the harbor. One big difference is the kind of ships that come in. They come from Canada, China, Japan, and Australia. There was even one from Chile the last time I was there. Silk. Rugs. Pottery. Amazing things."

"It does sound exotic and wonderful, Jeb, but I don't know. I don't know a single soul out there."

"Like I said. It's a friendly place. Give it a month, and you'll know plenty of folks."

As they approach the train station, she remembers something else he said. "What did you mean you have work to do first, before you land the long-term job? What kind of work?"

He looks a bit sheepish. "Well, it's like this. It's been two years since they passed an eight-hour workday law out there. But no one ever enforces it. And now the city's being flooded with new, cheap labor because every bum who can afford a train ticket has been heading west looking for work. At the docks, the shipowners will hire anyone to unload their cargo. Men are willing to work until they drop. They work ten-, twelve-, even fourteen-hour days. Sometimes they only pay them for eight, and the men say nothing. It's a big problem, and it needs to be sorted out."

She stops him and holds his chin in her hands, studying his healing wounds. "Another fight? Is that what you'll run into out there?"

"Maybe. Not a big one. But yes, it might get rough. If I help make things happen for the men, then the permanent union rep job is my reward."

She closes her eyes. "I can't, Jeb. I just can't. You might be able to live this way, but it tears me up to see you take risks and to see you hurt. And, the way you live makes me feel completely rootless. I could never drift the way you do."

He holds both of her hands, kissing them gently. "But you can for a while. You've come this far, haven't you? And you even enjoyed some of the trip! And I can still remember the look in your eyes when you helped me in Illinois. The way you handed me that bag as we fooled the cops. It was priceless. And you loved it. You know you did."

She smiles. "I loved being with you. I don't need exotic travel or danger to enjoy my time with you."

He kisses her hand. "But you do need to do what's right. I know that much about you. You know right from wrong, and you are very insistent on it."

She sighs and looks toward the clouds. "I'm glad that you think that, Jeb. But … well, it's just that I'm not sure what you do is right. I can't view it with the same passion as you do. To me, it's just gangs of men, looking for trouble with other gangs of men."

She walks to a shop window and looks in. But she doesn't really see what's in the wood and glass cases that stand in front of her. Jeb walks behind her and spoons up against her, kissing the back of her neck.

"I know it's a lot to think about right now. A lot to take in, and you and I haven't been together in weeks. You don't have to make your decision yet."

She nods.

He kisses her again. "First of all, thanks for staying. For staying here in this crazy place." He nuzzles closer. "Can you stay with me a while longer? Take the first part of the trip. To Montana at least. Commit to that maybe? It's a beautiful place."

She doesn't answer.

A shopkeeper emerges from the rear of the store and moves forward to stare at them through the window.

"We have to get out of this town, that's for sure," he laughs.

"I know."

She turns and hugs him, feeling the heat from his body through the layers of her starched dress.

"I'll go with you, Jeb. To Montana. At least that far."

He hugs her tightly. "You have to, Amanda. I don't want to lose you. Not after all of this. Not after all you've done for me."

Chapter 8

Old Building, New Life

On the north end of Cambridge, near the edge of the Mystic River, there sits a short row of decrepit brick buildings constructed sometime in the late 1700s. Originally built as large brick storage bins near a group of flour mills, the structures were later cut and modified with crude doors and windows, rough openings supported at their tops by iron plates bolted through the bricks.

Clearly utilitarian in their design, these buildings were not coveted as either business space nor as homes. They began their slow descent into disrepair sometime in the 1820s, once the water-powered flour mills closed, replaced by newer steam-driven plants located closer to town.

One of the old buildings was converted to a blacksmith shop around 1825, and it remained as such until the 1870s. Another served as an ice house. The others slowly collapsed once their roofs deteriorated.

The only major change for the two remaining buildings was the addition of a railroad track that runs along the buildings' north sides. For the next fifteen years, the ice house was used sporadically, but the former blacksmith shop sat nearly vacant, occupied only by mice, spiders, and a farmer up the road who kept his wagons there during the months when his own hay barn was filled.

When Victor Marius finally walks past the old blacksmith shop, he sees that the fronts of many of its bricks have started to crumble. The wall has seen too many seasons of freezing and thawing.

He walks around the building, banging on the walls and measuring their plumb lines. Despite the erosion, he finds that the walls are still solid enough and the roof seems fairly decent. Someone must have rebuilt it along the way. The foundation only leaks in the dead of winter, the owner says, and that can be fixed with a little new cement. A building like this has little value, and they both know it. After a bit of negotiation, Victor Marius is able to purchase it for just $120—as long as he agrees to take it as is and to pay cash.

It's nearly dusk when he stands inside, his freshly signed deed in hand.

His own place. Never did he dream his first piece of property would look like this.

The building looks nothing like a home. Not a neighbor in sight. It's little more than a decent-sized bare-bones chunk of covered space. Yet he couldn't be happier. This space is just the step back toward reality that he's been waiting to take.

Victor walks the perimeter of the large room. There's so much work to be done. Fifty years' worth of junk sits nearby. Rotting barrels and old barrel staves. Broken farm equipment. He sees a battered anvil from the building's blacksmith era that will probably stay right where it is because he couldn't lift it even if he wanted to. He looks toward a far corner and shakes his head in wonder. Is that the remains of a big foot-operated air bellows? It must be. And an empty coal bin too.

So much clutter. It could take days to clean this place. And he'd really rather be working on his idea for the electric fist.

But even amidst the squalor, he feels excitement that he hasn't felt in months. He feels fantastically alive, walking the space and dreaming of what will come. There are two lofts on either side of the main room. A set of stairs leads up to one. He could live in the loft on the left. There's enough room for a bed. The loft on the right can be reached only with a built-in ladder. A large wooden roof joist with a block and tackle hangs over the edge. Maybe he'll be able to haul his experimental generators up there once he builds them. Why not? Get them out of the way so that he has more floor space. Then he could build long workbenches along both walls. Yes. Yes, indeed. This space will do nicely.

And behind him is that wonderful train track. As one who supervises the installation of power lines, he knows that the lines will soon come through here along the side of the tracks. There's already a telegraph wire there, and his company has leased space on those poles for their electric wires. Electrical power and his backup generators. That alone will probably make the property in this area more valuable. So maybe he's made a wise investment.

And there, in the back, stands a small but sturdy lean-to addition with flat roof. It's one of the main reasons he purchased the building. He can walk out onto its roof from one of the lofts. It's the perfect place to set up a radio transmitter. And a receiver too. He can bolt the tower right to the roof.

Even with all the work that's still to be done, Victor decides to wait on the cleaning. He pulls out a pad of paper and makes some sketches. The tower would have to be at least thirty feet high. He'll need help bolting it into place.

One of the big problems he had in his earliest experiments was choosing a frequency for the transmission. So many other things could interfere with a signal. Any future test will probably have to cover a broader spectrum of the available frequencies.

Broad spectrum receiver? Has anyone coined that phrase yet? he wondered. No matter, that's what he will focus on next. Building that. Testing it.

Well, maybe he'd do that right after punching a few people with his battery-powered fist.

Chapter 9

Traction

Her mind is occupied with the images of soldiers. Thousands of soldiers. Each one stands ramrod straight, stretching to more than six feet tall and perfectly attentive. Each is lined squarely with other soldiers in a row that stretches on for miles and miles. But then she realizes there are even more. Behind the first row, there is another row, then another and another. The ranks of soldiers stretch into the vast distance until the perception of distance itself become incomprehensible.

She isn't quite asleep, but she feels herself jostled back toward consciousness as the train lurches.

It isn't really soldiers that Amanda has been seeing in her half-sleepy mind. It's rows of mid-summer corn stalks. The sameness of them, mile after mile out the train window, plays tricks on her vision. Hypnotic tedium and a barely changing landscape gives her mind leave to wander.

"Amazing, isn't it?" Jeb whispers over her shoulder.

"I was a farm wife once," Amanda says. "But I can't imagine ever working fields of this size. How can they do it?"

"They tell me that just ten years ago the fields weren't this large," he replies. "The farms were much smaller. But then the steam-driven traction engines came, and now the farmers out here can buy and plow and harvest as much as they want."

"What's a traction engine?" she asks. Whatever it is, she and Wayne never had one on their farm.

"They have names like Buffalo Pitts, Corliss, Rumely, Case … I've learned the names of some of the machine makers because I know their factories and their workers. They're expensive damn things, so when a farmer buys one, he has to know how to make the investment pay."

As Jeb talks, the huge cornfield comes to an end, replaced by a giant wheat field that seems to stretch on just as far.

"Since they have the space for it, some of the farmers around here just keep adding to their fields. Some have even bought out their neighbors and made farms that stretch for thousands of acres. The traction engines let them do it. You won't see the likes of that back in New England. There just isn't the space or the need for it."

Up ahead, they see about six men standing near the edge of the huge field. Looking over the ripe amber stalks, they all seem to be watching something. The train slows for a curve, and it gives Amanda and Jeb time to spot a shiny black machine. It is, indeed, one of the traction engines Jeb has been describing. As it makes its way rapidly up one side of the field, it pulls a threshing machine behind it.

Just as the train rounds a bend, the tractor, as some call it, rounds the edge of the field and pulls alongside the tracks.

"Well, look at that," Jeb says. He presses his face to the window, as do most of the other men in the car. "That's not a steam engine."

He points to the front of the machine. "That's a Rumely traction engine all right—I recognize it. But the whole water tank's been removed." He points to the back of the rig. "See? Look at that! Bolted onto the back of the frame. That's a damn gasoline engine!"

"The dickens you say …," a man in the seat ahead of them laughs. He opens the window and leans out to study the rig. "Why, look at that. That's just what it is, ain't it! Now where the hell do you suppose he got something like that?"

"Damned if I know," Jeb laughs.

"Germany." A man across the aisle says quietly. He's stepped out of his seat and is standing in the center aisle, trying to get his own look at the contraption. The other men stare at him.

"What do you mean 'Germany'?"

"Well, look at him. The man riding the thing. Blond hair. And look at the eyes and chin. He looks like a damn Hun, don't he?"

Jeb looks back toward the farmer, who is now heading away from them. "Well, maybe. But what difference does that make?"

"I'm from Hartford, Connecticut. Work for Steinway." The man sits back down in his seat, taking a stubby cigar out of his vest pocket. "That means I've seen a few gas engines in the past year or so."

The man in the seat ahead of Jeb looks confused. "What, the piano company?"

"Oh, Steinway," Jeb nods. "You guys are also getting into the engine business, right? You import them from Germany. I think I read that somewhere."

"Yes, that's just what we do," the man says as he lights his cigar. "From a small company called Daimler. That's why I know one of their engines when I see one. The Germans have been building gasoline engines for a good six years. My guess is that maybe someone in that farmer's family brought a gas-powered horseless carriage over with them when they moved to America. Krauts have been settling this area in recent years. That's got to be the story."

"Oh hell, that doesn't make sense," the man in the other seat scoffs. "Who could afford to ship something like that over here from Europe?"

"Good question. I don't have an answer for that, but there it is, engine made it here somehow. And it's bouncing along out there in that field."

Jeb laughs, then tries to make sense of it. "Okay, let's say that *is* how it got here. Maybe someone had a German automobile, and they just couldn't bear to leave it behind so they shipped it here. But why would they ever remove the engine? Why not keep the horseless carriage intact?"

The Steinway man points to a nearby dirt road. "Well, look at this place! There's nothing but rutted roads in these parts. Hard enough to drive a horse wagon here, much less something like that. Bet the carriage got busted apart. I don't see how it could have lasted very long driving around here. Besides, where are you going to get something like that repaired? Local wainwright might be able to fix the wheels and suspension, but damned if he'd be able to figure out how the power gets to the wheels. And how would he know how to fix a chain drive? Like I said, I'll bet it busted and that engine's all that's left of it."

All the men nod in quiet agreement.

"But, hey, hats off to him for finding another use for it. If I could stop the train, I think I'd run over there and offer to set him up in business. Steinway could sell him all the engines he can use. Hey, if he wants to turn 'em into farm traction engines, then why the hell not? That's his business."

Jeb laughs. "Jeb Thomas," he says to the other man, extending his hand in greeting.

Amanda gets up to take a walk, chased away by the acrid cigar smoke.

"Martin Lowery." The man grins and accepts the handshake.

"What brings you to this part of the country, Mr. Lowery? There's not much of a market for gasoline engines around here."

"Oh, I don't really deal in the engines. My main business is selling the pianos. I paid a visit to a few music stores in St. Louis and Kansas City. Now I'm headed to the frontier."

Jeb snorts. "Frontier? Where's that? There's no frontier left in this country anymore. The Wild West shows is all that's left of the frontier."

Lowery exhales a big puff of blue smoke. "Nonsense. I'm not talking about vast plains or Indians or even Buffalo

Bill. There's always a new frontier out there, my good man. It's just a matter of recognizing it when you see one."

"Is that a fact?"

The piano salesman takes another puff on his cigar and sizes Jeb up. He recognizes a well-traveled man when he sees one. Even though Jeb has not yet reached the age of thirty, he has wrinkles in the corners of his eyes, some gray at his temples, and he seems to exude the confidence of a man who's seen a lot, and who understands a lot.

"Tell me something, my good man. Did you see a frontier when you passed that field? Did you see those men looking at that contraption? Notice the look in their eyes?"

"I suppose I did," Jeb nods.

"That's a frontier, sir. A business frontier. If that contraption holds up, pretty soon all of those men will want a better traction engine in their barns. To hell with steam."

"A better engine."

"You bet your bottom dollar. It's coming. That farmer's little experiment was just a small hint of what's in store."

"I see," Jeb says with a hint of sarcasm. "So what's the frontier for pianos?"

"Oh, you'd be surprised. Every new mining town needs a saloon and a little music to go with it. Maybe a piano for the local hotel too. I also told my boss that I'd check to see if any miners or loggers needed engines too. Maybe that will end up being my new thing. I'll get a cut on that if I open up some new places for them to make a sale. Doesn't matter to me what I'm selling. I follow the need, and pianos can be iffy sometimes."

"You think there's a market for gas engines in the mines and other industries too?"

"Of course, there is!" He leans back in the tall upholstered chair. "Steam engines are big and heavy. Tough to haul them around and drag them to the bottom of a shaft. Then you have to shovel all that coal. Gas engines just have a line in. So … I'll do some checking. Who knows? Maybe I'll end up selling gasoline engines full-time. A sale is a sale, my good man."

Amanda stands on the rear deck of the last train car. Only the caboose is behind her. She thinks about the blond driver of the tractor, recalling that he had a look of pride on his face, but Amanda had noticed something else too. The only way she could describe it was a look of bored arrogance.

It was as if that farmer knew that he had the latest and greatest toy in town. The men standing at the edge of the field were obviously awed by it. But his success had brought with it a strange reward—more work. With better tools, his fields had merged and become so large that his modified traction engine looked like a small boat floating on an ocean of waving wheat.

His mission, to cut that wheat, seemed immense. His circles everlasting. The newness of his machine will wane, the crowds will go home, and he will be left alone in his huge field, doing a huge, dull task.

At that moment, Amanda realizes she could never go back to the farm life. It's a fine life for some, but it was never for her. It's too isolated. Too lonely.

Staring at the endless fields, she wonders if Wayne had sensed that in her. Had her discontent with the life she'd chosen with him eventually eaten away at him? Had affection been replaced with malice? Amanda had always blamed him for the way he was, but these fields, the endless toil, could have eaten away at him. All of this has brought back memories of how she too had changed once she moved to Wayne's farm.

Amanda stays on the back deck for a long time, until the sun reaches the ground and the flat fields fall away, replaced by rolling foothills. The sound of the train's engine changes as it climbs higher.

By the time they enter Colorado and cut across the square northeast corner of that state, she's returned to her seat, leaning against Jeb's shoulder.

"Tell me about this place," she whispers. "The place where we're going."

He shakes his head, as if describing it won't do it the justice it deserves.

"I need to know more about it," she insists.

"I'll try. But it's constantly changing. I haven't been there in eighteen months. It might not even be the same place when we get there. That's how wild and fast-growing it is."

He tells her how Butte was little more than a mining camp at the end of the Civil War. The miners had great hopes for gold and silver, and they found some, but it never rivaled the larger strikes found elsewhere.

"The big lodes were copper. But what could they do with copper? Military had some use for it. Copper was good for pennies and waterpipes too, but not much else. Didn't seem worth the mining effort to a lot of people."

He grins a mischievous grin. "But then something else came along, and suddenly the world has been looking for as much copper as they can get their hands on."

Amanda thinks for a moment, then smiles. "Wires!"

"Exactly. Copper electrical wires. Miles and miles of the stuff. Houses and factories and office buildings full of wires! For the past ten or so years, the mining towns of Montana have been some of the fastest-growing towns in the U.S. They might as well be pulling money right out of the dirt. Men have been wandering up here looking for work. Most of them usually find it. But I'll tell you, it can sometimes come at a hell of a cost."

"And that is?"

"Poisoned lungs. Greenish-orange chemicals embedded in your skin. Crushed arms and legs. Death from exhaustion because laws aren't obeyed. Butte has become a union town, mostly for its own safety, but there are always new men arriving and willing to work fast and loose. Willing to take a gamble. That makes it a real struggle to keep things safe."

"And that's why they need you?"

He nods. "There's a new contract coming due, and I'm just going to give the men a bit of advice on how to negotiate. That's all."

"Is it dangerous?"

"No more than Boston," he assures her with a kiss on the forehead. "Nothing happened there."

She leans her head against his shoulder as they sway back and forth. The train rises and falls over the foothills, chugging toward the distant mountains.

"I didn't know you got involved in mining too. You never mentioned it."

"Labor is labor," he says. "Actually, I usually stay away from mines if I can. Never like to go in them. Tight spaces seem to close in on me. Make me nervous. And I hate that." He looks at her with a sheepish smile. "I almost went crazy in that jail cell."

Amanda pulls him close, kisses him, then turns to watch the sunset. She's slowly lulled to sleep by the double *click clack* of the steel wheels as they roll northwestward throughout the night. Her mind is filled with images again, this time of bright polished copper and gleaming wires that stretch off toward the horizon.

Chapter 10

Marks

The business arrangement of Devlin Richards and Irene Fitzgerald may have emerged from the intersection of convenience and cravings, but it has settled into a partnership between a pair of profligate predators.

When the evenings are warm, especially during the workweek, Devlin takes a seat at the end of the bar. He has no interest in small talk with other patrons, though he will, on occasion, talk with one of the bartenders. What he does keep an eye out for is a slight nod from Irene. Her head tilts in the direction of a potential mark. A textile seller from Lowell. A cargo ship owner down from Prince Edward Island. A man from Connecticut who represents industrial machine parts.

Over the course of a week, Devlin follows them all – out into the night.

He and Irene have devised a simple formula. After the potential mark has completed his upstairs business, he usually is offered a last drink, on the house. As he sips at his liquor and savors his afterglow, Irene talks with the girl or girls who spent time with the gentleman. How thick was his wallet? Any gold? Fancy jewelry? Potential weapons?

Irene whispers a few words into Devlin's ear, and adds "No killing, you understand? No violence at all if you can help it. We don't need the police sniffing around."

Then Devlin slips out the side door, ready for the mark to emerge from the front of the house. As the mark walks away, Devlin follows.

The first few robberies go off without a hitch. Devlin usually waits for the right moment, accosts the gentleman, and slams him up against a wall. The impact alone is enough to frighten most men, and they quickly hand over their valuables. One of the men tries to strike him with a cane, but Devlin slaps it away and shows him his knife. The man's eyes widen and they quickly finish their exchange.

But the forth attack doesn't go as smoothly. The target, this time a lawyer from Albany, takes a quick swing and makes a lucky connection with Devlin's cheek. Devlin blocks a second blow, only to realize it was a fake. The man kicks him hard in the shin, and as he bends a bit, clips him hard with an elbow to the side of the head.

That's enough to stoke a burning rage in Devlin. He responds with a series of close-in punches to the man's head and chest. The man tries to pull a gun from his coat pocket, but with the barrage of blows, it ends up clattering to the paving stones. Devlin gives him a mighty shove, then bends down, picking up the gun.

"This bullet meant for me? Hum?" He holds the barrel just inches from the man's face. "Now it's meant for you."

The lawyer looks at the gun, and at Devlin, with equal parts defiance and fear.

Devlin feels a trickle of blood running down his cheek. That first blow must have cut him. "Empty your pockets. Maybe you'll live, maybe you won't. Do it now."

The man from Albany does so, dropping a wallet, a gold chain and some cufflinks onto the ground.

"Now the coat."

Again, the man drops what he is told to drop. In response, Devlin pistol whips him hard on his collar bone. The man grunts and slumps forward, but Devlin turns him, kicks him in the ass and sends him down the street. The southerner smiles with satisfaction as he sees the lawyer stumble away, holding his broken bone.

Irene is already waiting in her suite when Devlin returns. She rushes to him, brushing back his hair. "What happened to your cheek?" she asks.

"Occupational hazard."

She kisses him hard, then licks the blood with a savage smile.

The take from this evening's marks turns out to be their best of the week. The wallet contains over $160. The cufflinks and chain (no watch attached, unfortunately) look like solid gold. Then there's the pistol. It's a Forehand & Wadsworth. English Bulldog style with snub nose. Fancy engraving along the handle. Classy gun all the way.

Irene locks the booty away in her desk and leads Devlin over to her bed. She licks his cut again and compliments him on his good work, on how tough he is.

She also shows him some of the other perks of his new job.

Chapter 11

Cages

The policeman walks through the back door of his station, offering little more than a grunt to a pair of other officers who sit at a small white table. He quickly heads down a long hallway, toward the dark rooms located near the middle of the building.

He twirls the waxed ends of his mustache as he walks. Looks nervously over his shoulder.

"You know him?" one of the cops at the table asks the other. Eyes follow the other police officer down the hall.

"Not really. His name's Hudson, I think. From the next precinct over. Pretty much keeps to himself."

They both shrug and go back to their newspapers and cups of tea.

The dark rooms are both locked, but Hudson has managed to procure a key. Looking up and down the hallway, he slips the key into the lock on the door of the room. Moving quietly, he lets himself in.

One of the policemen in the break room looks up. "What was that?" He tries to peer down the dark hallway but can't quite see all the way to the rooms.

"Did he go into the lockup?"

"Sounded like he did. So what?"

"Just that a lot of stuff has been missing from there lately."

"Yeah? Well, that don't mean nothin'. He's probably just locking up something he took off some thief."

"You think so? Now you tell me—you ever seen Hudson, or whatever his name is, haul in anybody or anything? Either here or over in his own precinct? I don't even know what he does. Just walks the streets, I think. From what I've seen, he don't act like a cop at all."

"Bah," the other policeman grunts. "Who knows? You're new here. Takes a while to get it all figured out."

"Yeah. Guess you're right." And with that, he goes back to his newspaper.

Once inside the room, Officer Hudson relocks the door from the inside, then slips out a candle and matches from his pocket. In a few moments, he has enough light to prowl around, and he makes his way up a short row of tables. Seeing nothing of interest, he looks underneath, spending several minutes loading and unloading the contents of various boxes.

"Nuthin!" he mutters to himself. But he does find a very nice pewter snuff box with scrollwork on the top. With a smile, he slides it into his coat pocket.

To his right he sees a safe. He's never seen it before, but figures it must be the one that was removed from Chen Lu's backroom. Several holes and dents along the front indicate that the lock mechanism has been drilled out. He yanks the door open but finds the safe barren inside.

"Fuck."

Next he turns his attention to a row of wire lockers near the back wall. A sign hanging over the middle group declares: "Evidence lockup. Do not remove any items."

But the lockup doesn't really lock. While iron bars slide down the right edge of each column, all the lockers can be accessed by simply removing the bars.

Hudson does this once, twice, three times, searching through the stacks of lockers, and then replacing each bar. The fourth time, he finds something interesting.

It's a burlap sack. Hefting it, he can feel something about the size of a shoebox inside, but considerably heavier. A light tap tells him that it's wood.

He quickly opens the bag and looks inside. Yes. This must be it.

Pulling it out, he looks at the box in the flickering light. It's just as Devlin Richards described it. Inlaid wood and all.

Chapter 12

The Great Bear

In the morning, Amanda and Jeb switch trains in Cheyenne then spend most of the day traversing the high plains and rugged hills of northern Wyoming. Eventually they cross into southern Montana. The view is breathtaking.

Salesman Martin Lowery continues to travel with them. He's expressed interest in visiting some mining towns to judge their need for his strange combination of internal combustion engines and pianos. "Might as well be Butte that I visit, eh?" he says. "That place is growing faster than any other mining town, and I can ride along with you folks."

Jeb gives him a smug look. "Does the fact that you may find your potential customers at local drinking establishments and bawdy houses have anything to do with the products you represent?"

Lowery just winks in reply.

The sun hasn't quite set, but it's definitely evening by the time they pull into Butte. Again, chased away by the swirling cigar smoke in the passenger car, Amanda stands this time on the front platform of the first car, located just behind the locomotive and the coal car. In the still evening air, the train's black smoke and glowing embers sink low. Luckily there's just enough breeze to push the smoke to the right side of the train as she stands slightly to the left. The only thing she can see straight ahead is a mound of coal and, thirty feet beyond that, the locomotive's fat black smokestack. She's ever mindful of the soot and sparks that fly nearby. Her penchant for standing in harm's way has already cost her one perfectly good dress on this trip.

Butte is not at all what she expected. In her mind, she's pictured wonderful steep hills and a picturesque village, similar to the photos she's seen of other Western towns. She had expected broad main streets and neat wooden shops with a bustle of people coming and going.

Here, all the buildings are brick or stone. Here, a man-made cloud hangs over the city. Jeb warned that she would see smelters on the outskirts of the town. She can't quite see them yet, but she sees what they produce: a different kind of smoke, greenish-brown and greasy-looking. These clouds hang low over the tracks and over the town itself. When the train crosses a small creek, the water is the strangest shade of green she's ever seen. It's as if someone has mixed milk and clothing dye and poured it onto the landscape. On the far bank, she sees a dead mallard lying next to the jade-like water.

The train station is tiny and nearly empty when they arrive. She sees only a ticket agent and a man slumped on a metal bench. As they gather their things and head toward the street, the bench-bound loiterer gives out an occasional wheezy cough.

"I don't have any idea where I should stay," Lowery remarks. He sticks by them as Jeb and Amanda walk up the street.

"Well, we're going to the Great Bear Hotel," Jeb tells him. "But I'm afraid it won't be through the front door."

Amanda wasn't aware that they were sneaking into a hotel. Her apprehension grows with each step. Jeb notices.

"Now, now," he says, arm around her shoulder, "all the arrangements have been made. A good friend has set us up with a wonderful large room on the top floor."

"If you say so."

Jeb glances at Lowery, as if to judge how his words will be interpreted by this man, whose political persuasion is unknown to him.

"It's just that this is a company town," he whispers to Amanda. "The hotel is owned by the same folks who own the largest mine. I'm not exactly welcome there, but the same desk clerk who might turn us away when people are watching is also enough of a friend to make sure we're invited to the back door and made comfortable when no one is looking."

Lowery says nothing, but continues to walk with them.

"You want to make some sales here?" Jeb asks

"I wouldn't be here if I didn't," Lowery grunts. He's obviously packed too heavy, and he's growing winded, hauling his suitcase on their walk down Wyoming Street.

"Let me give you some advice then. You might want to try selling the engines instead of the pianos. Industry is growing. No new hotels or brothels here for the past two years. The men you want to talk to are the mine foremen. Also, talk to the track boss. Talk to the dock boss. They're the ones who make sure things keep moving. You sell them, and they'll in turn sell the mine owners. Your only real selling point is how much ore they can move, and how much money can be made."

Lowery puffs and nods.

"Those men need to move product, and that product is ore. They need to move it out of the pick rooms, down the main street—that's what they call the central tunnel, you know, the main street—and then the ore goes up the shaft. Heavy as hell to lift. They're using mules now, with pulleys and fucking long, long ropes. And, occasionally, some steam engines. But a steam engine only comes into play if they can lower one down the shaft and then only if they have a way to vent the smoke and not kill everyone in the process."

"Our internal combustion engines make smoke too, of course."

"Well, then I guess you need to convince them it makes less smoke. Safer smoke that's easier to vent."

As they reach downtown Butte, they cross a wide alley that seems to pulse with accordion music and loud voices. Planks are stretched across the front and sides of the alley, making it look like a barn with no roof. An empty whiskey bottle sails over the front fence, smashing on the street in front of them. The crash startles a passing horse, who rears up with a loud snort. The horse's rider, seemingly conditioned to such interruptions, expertly reins the horse under control and back down. The stallion spins in a circle and finally settles as the rider pats his neck.

"Watch out, ya damn fool!" the rider shouts at the alley, then rides on. Inside the fence, a man swears back at him as a woman giggles.

Jeb, Amanda, and Lowery stop to look at the fence boards. "What is this place?" Lowery asks.

"Venus Alley," Jeb laughs. "They've got women in there, parked in a long set of stalls, just like veal calves."

"You've got to be kidding," says Amanda. She clutches Jeb's arm.

"It's a whore house?" Lowery asks with amazement.

"Not really a house at all, is it?" Jeb says as he studies the crowd inside the alley. They can see over a dozen people through the narrow front gate. "Amazing. It's much bigger than the last time I was here. But, yes, that's what it is, all right. A sort of outdoor cat house." He starts to walk toward the fence for a better look, but Amanda holds him back.

"Guess these girls couldn't get work in the fancier places," Jeb continues. "So they're sort of self-employed out here. I don't know if anyone actually owns the alley. The stalls and beds, such as they are, are built by anyone who can swing a hammer."

Lowery just stares, dumbfounded. A plain-faced redhead with a low-cut dress peeks over the fence and winks at him. Lowery looks flustered and turns to leave.

They walk on in silence until Amanda finally whispers in Jeb's ear. "Well, if things don't work out, I suppose I could always find work back there!"

He laughs. "I think you could do much better than being a stall girl in that alley, my dear. You're top-quality material."

"I'll take that as a compliment. I think."

They split up near the front porch of the Great Bear Hotel, with Lowery going inside to check in at the front desk as Jeb and Amanda continue around to the back. Jeb taps a special two-three-two knock. A woman with a cigarette dangling from her lips opens the back door. She's dressed in men's clothes and carries a revolver in her hand.

"And you want what there, cowboy?"

"I'm expected," Jeb replies.

"You Jeb Thomas?" she asks, lips barely moving.

"That I am."

"Yeah, well, come in. Nick said you'd be here. Hope you know I expected you a good two hours ago."

Jeb slides into the narrow crack as she steps back from the door. Amanda hesitates, then follows.

"I apologize," he said. "I didn't know the train schedule when I sent him the cable."

She accompanies them up a narrow back stairs and escorts them into a room that's been set up as a makeshift parlor. It's apparently where she lives, with an attached bedroom at the back.

"Nick's out. Over at the Dumas Hotel, the damn fool. Said to put you folks up in the top floor. Nick must like you if he wants you to stay there. He's got other places in town too."

"Nick and I go way back," Jeb smiles. "To the days of his first copper strike, when he sold his claim to Daly. Made Nick rich, though part of the deal was that he had to stay on and supervise."

The woman, who hadn't introduced herself, looks Jeb up and down. "And that's the only reason he likes you, ya know. If he'd of stayed an owner, I doubt he'd have much use for a little union shit like you."

Jeb simply smiles and nods, squeezing Amanda's hand when he senses she's about to come to his defense.

"Okay, upstairs it is then. Thanks for letting us in."

They head back to the stairway, but the woman calls after them.

"Oh, one more thing. The meeting you were supposed to have out at the number five shaft tomorrow? Nick says you have to have it tonight. Some of Daly's top men are going to be out there tomorrow. Wouldn't be good for you to be there. He needs to talk with you before then."

"Tonight? Shit." Jeb rubs his eyes.

"Yeah, well, that's how it is. Know how to get there?"

"I do."

"Then the problem is yours, not mine, union boy. See you later." She shuts the door abruptly. Even through the door's thick pine panels, Amanda can hear the woman take another drag on her smoldering tobacco.

Jeb seems nervous as they climb the stairs. After they light the lamp, they see that the upstairs room is quite large, perhaps 20 by 15 feet. The top story of the hotel is smaller than the other levels, so their space takes up maybe 25 percent or so of what is essentially the third floor. At the end of the room near the door, a thick down mattress sits upon an iron frame with a scrolled headboard and footboard. The metal is painted a delicate blue, but the color is starting to show its age, faded on the window side and peeling near the curled feet. A patchwork quilt covers its puffy surface. There are a few loose threads here and there, but Amanda is impressed by the quality of its fabric.

"This is actually a decent hotel," Jeb says. "I don't think they rent out the third floor rooms very often, so the older stuff sort of migrates up here."

At the far end of the room are two more windows with yellowing lace curtains. A small round table with a stained doily sits between, as do two straight-backed chairs.

"This must have been a delightful place at one time," Amanda says, mostly to herself.

"Yeah, well, a woman's touch is hard to find in a town like this. Miners come and go, and most would just as soon sleep in a barn as a fancy hotel."

They quickly unpack and pay a visit to the little room across the hall. There's no lamp inside the bath, so Jeb searches through the empty rooms until he finds one. The space offers little more than a chamber pot under a chair with an open seat. The washing area is an old dry sink with a big white bowl on top. A cold water spigot juts from the wall above, so at least they have that. There is no drain. They simply pour the bowl out the window.

Then Jeb gets ready to leave.

"I don't understand why you have to go out there tonight," Amanda says. "Why can't it wait until morning?"

"Best time to meet with my union guys is when fewer people are around. On the night shift, everyone is a working man."

He can see the look of concern in her eyes.

He offers additional reassuring words as he dons a clean shirt. "It will take me a while to get out to the mine and back, and my meeting will be maybe thirty minutes or so."

"I'm not staying here alone. I don't like this place, or that woman."

He shakes his head. "You can't come with me. The mine's a dangerous place, and you'll be the only woman."

"I don't care. I feel more vulnerable right here." She looks up at him. "Besides, I can tell you're nervous. You really don't want to go inside the mine, do you?"

"Like I said. I'll be fine."

"I know you will, because I'll be with you."

Jeb shakes his head, but he knows better than to argue. "All right then, but put on a pair of my pants and roll up the cuffs. There's no way you'll get up that hill wearing one of your dresses."

Chapter 13

The Weight

Ever since he moved to his new laboratory, which is also his new home, Victor has spent most of his energy clearing, cleaning, and rebuilding the structure. Making it useful. Making it right.

If everything goes well, this big space will become the focal point of his work and his life.

But even with the mountain of chores he needs to tackle, there is still a burning vigor inside of him. It's something that can't be quenched with work alone.

The scientist knows the chief catalyst for the yearning and the energy he feels is the elixir he's been injecting. But he doesn't mind that at all. The concoction keeps his battery fully charged. It forces him to find ways to burn off the excess resolve. This unlocked energy is how he's managed to rebuild his muscles so far.

And, he does wonder, just how far can he push that?

His makeshift barbell, with the heavy brass gears from the old bell tower, sits near the broad front door of his lab. Every morning and evening, he picks up the rig and curls it toward his chin, lifting it repeatedly – to the point of exhaustion.

His muscles always protest at first. Then they do their work and resignedly break down, only to slowly repair themselves and grow ever so slightly larger over the next day or two.

Bigger. Ever bigger.

For the evening workout, it's a fair night with a light breeze from the south. New vines have grown high on the fence across the street, and right outside his door – honeysuckle. Tiny flowers, with the same varying shades of yellow and tan found in the evening clouds, release their sweet aroma into the air.

Victor stares through the doorway and completes the last five repetitions with the big weight. Trance-like, he forces the gears upward. His muscles burn.

Stronger indeed. He's never done this many reps before.

In his hyper-focused state, he doesn't hear the distant cry at first. But as he lowers the weight for the last time, a desperate voice catches his ear. It's a cry for help, coming from just a hundred or so feet away.

Victor steps outside, and sees a man dragging a woman, who has fallen to her knees, along the rough gravel of the street. It takes a moment for him to realize the man is yanking on a beaded purse that's attached to the belt of the woman's dress by a brass chatelaine. The thief can't quite rip the purse free due to the decorative chains that hold it in place.

"You there!" Victor takes a step forward. But the thief yanks harder, with a new urgency, lifting the woman from the ground. The chains break. The woman, stout of body and hampered by her layers of clothes, thuds to the ground with a grunt. Her dark hair, streaked with grey, unfurls from its bun. Keys and a small pair of scissors fall from the chains as the thief turns, intending to flee down the street.

Victor longs to give chase, but he hesitates. With sudden inspiration, he turns to look at his big barbell. The street has a slight slope to it, and the thief is heading down the hill. Decision made, Victor quickly picks up the rig, steps to the middle of the street, and lines the thief up in his sights. With a mighty shove, he sends the barbell rolling down the middle of the thoroughfare.

Lurching and bobbing along the gravel, the teeth of the gears seem to bite hard against the ground, keeping the axle on a steady path. The weight helps it gain momentum.

The thief, trying to run faster, hears the sound of something approaching. He looks over his shoulder but can't quite comprehend what this thing is that's coming after him. He only knows that it's gaining.

He stumbles a bit as he reaches an intersection, but regains his stride and tries to turn the corner.

It's too late. The heavy rig mows the man down. He falls hard, face first in a cloud of dust. The rig bounces up his back and the left gear rides up, ripping his clothes and smacking him hard in the back of the head.

After doing its work, the barbell rolls on, until it comes to rest in some tall weeds near the base of the railroad tracks.

The thief does not get up again. He's out cold.

Victor helps the crying woman to her feet and together they walk to where the man lies to retrieve her purse. In a halting breath, she explains that she is the head housekeeper for a Beacon Hill family. She's only passing through the industrial neighborhood because it's a convenient cut-through to a Saturday evening farmers' market, the one that's set up between the bridges on the bank of the Charles.

"Thank you, sir. Thank you so much. The Misses would be so angry if I lost the money she gave me for meat, eggs, and butter."

Victor picks up the purse, pats the woman on her shoulder and sends her on her way. Then he looks at the man on the ground. He nudges him with his foot, and hears the thief groan.

"You'll live." Victor laughs.

But the words sound disturbingly familiar, and he realizes he's amassed a string of devious wins. This victory, in particular, rings hallow. It wasn't one-on-one. It wasn't close in. It was a smart mind outwitting muscle.

He decides not to contact the police. Let the man lay here and sleep it off on the gravel. Let him awaken and realize just what his deed cost him.

Turning his attention to his barbell, Victor pulls the rig from the weeds and sets it in the street. Sucking in a couple of deep breaths, he picks it up and takes the first steps of a 200-foot journey back up the small hill to the door of his lab.

Chapter 14

Lost & found

"I don't care what you say." The patrolman in the break room looks at his friend with derision. "That man just took something out of the lockup. I'm sure of it."

The other cop looks uninterested. "So what if he did? He must have his reasons." He looks at the younger officer like the man is a rank amateur.

"One of the first things they taught us when I came on board is that you don't take anything out of that room without first telling the duty officer. Right? Didn't you learn that too?"

"Shit, how long have you been here, lad? A month?"

"Just about."

"You've got to get used to the way things work. There's the official rules, and then there's the way things are done. The two sets of rules don't always join up perfectly. Know what I'm saying?"

The young patrolman, whose name is Sam Everett, nods. And he might even be willing to accept those words, except that Hudson, the cop who walked away with a burlap sack under his arm, is not at all trustworthy. In Everett's eyes, Hudson isn't someone who's bending the rules a bit. He's outright breaking them, and boldly walking past his coworkers while doing so.

Everett stands and walks toward the hallway.

"Where the hell are you going?"

"Going to talk to the duty officer."

"God damn it, Sam!" says his friend. "You're going to cause a rift. You know that? That's what comes from complaining. You're so hell-bent that you're right. What if you ain't?"

But Sam Everett keeps walking, right past Patrolman Hudson, who looks at him with disdain.

"Hey," Everett calls out as he approaches the duty officer's desk, "did Hudson sign anything out of the lockup?"

"Huh? Let's see … Hudson … Hudson …." The duty officer shuffles through a stack of papers, obviously caught daydreaming.

"Never mind the name. Did anyone sign anything out?"

"Tonight? No. Not a soul. Been pretty quiet."

Everett points down the hallway. He hears quick footsteps heading toward the back door. "Well, guess what? Someone was just in the lockup. One of our own, sort of. Named Hudson. And he took something."

"Well, okay …," the duty officer says, like that's the end of the discussion.

"If he didn't sign it out, you're supposed to stop him. You're supposed to challenge anyone who doesn't do things by the book."

"Well, yeah … but …."

"But what?"

The officer shakes his head. "God damn it. Okay. Fine."

As the duty officer heads down the hallway, Everett decides to head out the front door in order to circle around to the back. He quickens his pace as he reaches the side of the building.

"Hey, what do you have there?" he demands as he sees Hudson trot through the alley.

"What? Who the hell are you?" Officer Hudson clutches the sack closer and keeps on walking.

"You didn't sign that out. The duty officer needs to talk with you. I think he's coming around from the back door."

"I don't know what you're talking about. Get the fuck out of the way."

Hudson starts to nudge past Officer Everett just as the duty officer rounds the corner and spots the pair. "Hey, hang on there!" he calls.

Hudson starts to run, knocking Everett down in the process. What he doesn't count on is Sam Everett's partner, who has wandered out of the break room to watch events unfold. Whether he agrees with the proceedings or not, Hudson has just knocked down his friend, so he decides it's finally time to act. He makes a grab, yanking the bag from Hudson's hands.

"Well, well, what have we here? You running like that makes me wonder if my buddy was right about you."

"It's nothing. … I can explain," Hudson stammers.

"No need to explain to me—explain to him," he points to the duty officer. "And since he's going to have to protect his ass, I'm sure he'll tell his boss that you did everything without his permission. I'm going to love hearing you explain your way out of this one."

Chapter 15

Motherlode

The town of Butte seems bright and lively, but the road out of town toward the mine grows dark tremendously fast. It's not a long ride, but Amanda feels like she's been pulled up into the night sky as they bump along. Darkness swallows all. There is no moon, but at least the stars seem bright. The sky is a black canvas with white pinholes stretching over the road, the wagon, and the scrubby trees.

In fifteen minutes, they reach a group of huts. Lamplight spills from windows. Jeb climbs down and walks toward the larger hut, looking through the window before knocking on the door.

"Yeah?" a voice calls from inside.

"Barney around?"

"Who needs to know?"

Jeb clears his throat. "A guy who's supposed to meet with him."

The door opens a crack, and a gray-haired man peeks out.

"That you, Jeb?"

"Do I know you?"

"You sure do. Christ, what are you doing out here?"

Their voices drop to a whisper, but it's obvious to Amanda that Jeb is well known in these parts.

"Barney's over at shaft five. You can go see him there if you want, but don't you make no fuss 'round here tonight, you understand? We don't need that."

"I'm in and out like a ghost. You got my word on it."

Jeb returns to the wagon and turns the horses toward the shaft entrance, which stands about 300 feet away.

"Where are we going, Jeb?" Amanda asks, her voice harboring a nervous lilt.

"Quick meeting. You're staying here in the wagon."

"You know I said I'm not going to stay alone."

"Don't be crazy! This is a copper mine! You can't go down there with me."

"Then neither should you! It's dangerous. It's the middle of the night, Jeb!"

"Oh, for God's sake. It's always nighttime in a mine. They've got lanterns and there's probably forty men down there!"

She clings tightly to his arm as the wagon draws near the entrance. "I don't care. If you go, I'm going with you."

"I can't take a woman down a mine shaft."

"Why not?"

"Well, because … I mean … it just isn't done. You know that very well."

Even if she does know it, she isn't going to accept being left in an open wagon on a dark night. She continues to protest until Jeb acquiesces. They make their way toward the opening of the shaft, which is basically a very tall barn built over an opening in the ground. The height accommodates the steep slope plus a lift and some hoists.

The front is open, its doorway twice as large as an average barn door. There's one big room, and in the middle sits a vast iron frame. Amanda guesses that the frame probably started as a cube of girders measuring twenty feet per side. But other girders, with slightly different shades of black, were added to the sides of the cube. From each of these appendages dangles a special piece of gear. They appear to be specialty tools whose purposes are difficult to decipher. Each can be swung over the opening and dropped in as needed. There's also a large hoist that's probably used to lift the small rail cars, six by four feet, up and out of the hole. Those cars are used to haul copper ore through the tunnels.

Another beam supports a cage. Still another holds a claw device that looks like it belongs in a medieval torture chamber. To one side of the room sits a steam engine. Big as a locomotive, but without wheels, it hisses and chugs away. A huge flywheel sits alongside the engine. The wheel helps drive a wide leather belt that extends into the ground.

Even with the engine running, the flywheel sits idle, apparently disengaged, while the men below focus on another task.

Jeb holds her hand as they approach two men who stand near the top of the hole. They're looking down and struggling with a cable that drops into the vast emptiness below.

"No, no!" one of them shouts to an unseen colleague far below. "Spin her around! Well, yes, you have to! Damn it, she'll hit her head if I lower her any more!"

His exasperation grows. "Well, get a fucking pole or something and reach up to push her! I ain't going to bash her head again!"

The man turns to look at Jeb and Amanda. Since she's wearing men's clothing, it takes him a moment to realize he's looking at a woman. He's immediately embarrassed by his profanity.

"Oh, I … um …." He removes his grubby hat. "Sorry, ma'am." He appears confused as he looks her up and down. A lovely woman's face looks back at him. But it's strange to see such a woman in a flannel work shirt. She also wears pants, gathered in folds at the waist and rolled up at the cuffs.

The other worker lies on his belly and reaches into the shaft, poking at the cable with a Y-shaped stick. He seems far less concerned. He takes one look at Amanda, spits a huge wad of tobacco and juice into the hole, then turns back to his task.

These are the roughest-looking men Amanda has ever seen. There isn't an unsoiled patch anywhere on their clothes, and dark grime is caked into the wrinkles of their faces. It makes them look coarse as cowhide and impossibly old.

The miner who had been barking orders looks like he might have at least a veneer of civility, but it's buried under the gritty weight of time and circumstance. The man on his belly looks much more primitive, as if he may have once given some thought to courtesy and manners, but then rejected both as a waste of time.

"What the fuck do you two want?" he demands, pushing himself into a sitting position. And staring at Jeb.

"I have a meeting with your foreman," Jeb says confidently.

"Tony? Well, he's a might busy at the moment."

"I'm sure he is, but I believe he's expecting me."

"Oh yeah? Expecting her too?" the man looks toward Amanda. "Least I think it might be a 'her.' Not quite sure what you got in that outfit."

Both of the miners laugh.

Far below, they hear the braying of a mule. It sounds weak and terrified.

"Well," the sitting man continues, "excuse me if we don't give a shit at the moment. We have a mule halfway down the shaft. The sling makes it hard for her to breathe, and we need to spin her a bit to get her to fit."

The more polite of the two men points to the cage that dangles off the big iron frame. "If you want to meet with Tony, you'll find him at the bottom. You can go down if you want, but we can't lower you right now. We're using the main rig, and it's going to be a while."

"You're saying we can get down in that?" Jeb nods toward the cage. "How?"

"You'll have to lower yourself using the hand crank inside the escape cage."

Jeb is silent for several moments. He walks to the enclosure, which looks like little more than an enlarged bird cage. "How does it work?"

"Fits two men, or in your case, whatever," he laughs. "If you look down, you'll see that another small shaft's been cut right beneath it. Just get in. See the hand crank? Use it to lower yourself right down."

Jeb approaches the cage with apprehension. His dislike of small spaces gnaws at him. Amanda whispers to him as they walk. "What does he mean by a mule? A real mule?"

"Yes," Jeb replies. "They use them to pull the ore carts along a track down there. They have to lower them down to the bottom."

"And they stay down there?"

"Yes. Sometimes for months at a time."

Amanda thinks about this for a moment. "Goodness, that must smell wonderful after a while."

"Doesn't smell any worse than the miners themselves," Jeb laughs, trying to take his mind off the task at hand.

He peers into the cage. His hand grows sweaty.

"It's fine," Amanda whispers in his ear. "I'm right here with you. Get in."

They climb inside and shut the door. He closes his eyes and starts turning the crank. Slowly they descend through the roughly circular slot in the ground. Amanda has a troubling image in her mind. It's like being a sardine trapped in a can. But it's worse than that. It seems as if the entire can is being swallowed by a giant worm.

For the first several feet there is nothing but rock beside them. It's nearly pitch black, but there's enough light coming from above and below that they can see the walls of their rock tube. They watch the walls slide by, like they're inside the worm's esophagus. Amanda clutches Jeb by his waist. Eventually the tube grows brighter as they go down.

"We must have dropped a good sixty-five feet," Jeb says, "and still more to go."

He feels tired, and they stop to rest for a moment. A feeling of panic seeps in for both of them. It's hard work to get down, and it will be harder still to get back up. But if they don't resume their exhausting effort, they're stuck in the middle. Rock seems to close in from all sides.

"Can you do more?" Amanda asks, stroking his hand.

"I think so."

"I'll help."

There's no room in the cage for them to reposition, so she reaches around from behind, chest pressed against his back. Together they crank again.

The light continues to brighten, and they finally emerge into an underground room that is roughly 60 by 70 feet. Still dangling thirty feet from the bottom, they now can see the mule beside them, still dangling and clearly distraught. The mule spins a bit, and Amanda and Jeb come face-to-face with her. The animal's eyes seem to glow green, looking right at them. It takes a moment for Amanda to realize the eyes are just reflecting the light from a torch on the wall behind them.

Four men stand at the bottom of the shaft. All of them stop to watch the cage slowly drop the rest of the way to the floor. One of them laughs as the cage door opens and Jeb stumbles out, looking tired and stressed.

"You don't look so good there, partner!"

Jeb says nothing and starts to look for his contact, Tony, eventually spotting him near the opening to the long main tunnel. For the moment, Tony looks like the mayor of some decrepit Main Street.

He nods hello and walks over to talk with Jeb. Their voices are hushed. It's a private, divisive conversation. Voices rise and fall, and Amanda does not feel welcome to listen. Instead she watches as the mule descends her final few feet, twisting in a slow circle and letting out a mighty "Hawwwww" as she reaches the floor.

The men unhook the sling. They seem more interested in calling up to the men above than paying attention to the animal. The mule stumbles out of the way, barely noticed. Amanda approaches her, feeling the animal shiver and shrink away from her touch.

"Shhhh, it's okay," she tells her. "It's okay. You're safe."

"Be careful. She'll bite-cha. She will!" one of the workers hollers. His gap-tooth smile seems both friendly and a bit crazed. "Take your finger plumb off. Happened to a friend a mine!"

He laughs a little private laugh, then looks her up and down before turning back toward the ropes.

The animal eventually lets Amanda touch her face. Long slow strokes along her neck and ears seem to soothe her. With nothing else to do and no desire to chat with the men, she continues to make friends with the mule. She can hear Jeb and Tony in the background.

"I'm telling you, your plan ain't going to work." The voice belongs to Tony, and it rises from the left side of the stone room. Words, once spoken, have nowhere to go amongst the rocks, so they bounce and curve around the walls until the sounds find their way into all ears, no matter how softly one speaks.

"There's too many folks in the town now," Tony continues. "They got miners waiting for work everywhere. If I try to pull a work slowdown right now, they'll fire us all. They'll do that sure as hell."

"So that's it?" Jeb asks. "Just going to quit the fight?"

"What the hell choice do we have but to take the wage cut, Jeb? I ain't going to go jobless. Neither are most of my men."

"You've got a union here, Tony. You've got more power in this situation than you think. It takes skill to mine copper the right way, doesn't it? You *know* it does."

Tony waves Jeb off and walks back toward the center of the room. "Tell that to the damn Chinamen," he says. "More of them coming every day. You tell that to them, because they're my biggest problem here now."

Jeb nods, well aware of the issue.

The wild, toothless man who warned Amanda about the mule decides to join the conversation. "Yes, indeed. Just like he say. They's coming up from the railroads," he snarls. "Not as much work for 'em there anymore, I guess. The Irish is coming too, though not as many. I think most of them micks head back east when they's done pounding spikes."

The ropes and the mule sling, now bundled together, rise slowly and disappear up into the darkness. A moment later, something dings and clangs down from above. Whatever it is, it crashes to the floor, landing with a metallic bounce. Amanda looks down and sees a large iron wrench that could easily have killed someone if it had landed on their head.

"Sorry!" a voice calls out from far above.

"Will you fucking watch what you're doing up there!" Tony shouts.

The gap-tooth miner walks over to take the mule from Amanda. "I got to get this lady hooked up. You can come along if you want, girly boy, but we's got lots a' work to do, yes, indeedy."

Amanda hesitates, then decides to follow, partly out of concern for the animal, and partly out of curiosity to see where the Main Street leads. Jeb stays behind, still talking with Tony.

With the light of a torch to guide them, they walk a short way down the main hall. There are more torches ahead. Amanda sees several more men, some dirt-black, some with greenish dust on them, some with shavings of bright copper hanging from their hair. Several of them are dragging wooden boxes out of side corridors and dumping their contents into the ore cars that sit on a small track. There are more mules and donkeys here, tied to short groups of carts. When a couple of carts are filled, the mules haul them toward the main shaft as the next group of mules and carts step up to take their place.

The air smells foul with a combined stench of torch smoke, sweat, and the waste of both animals and men. There's another smell too, lingering behind the more noticeable orders. It's the smell of the earth—deep, rich, and carrying a hint of sulfur.

"What you got there, Lucas?" one of the miners calls out.

"Just a new pack mule is all. They just sent her down."

"So I see!" The minor laughs and points to Amanda. "Nice a ya to bring two of 'em!"

She hears snickering and turns to see other men, faces dirty, knuckles bleeding, lurking in the shadows. All eyes are on her.

"She looking to be a miner too?" someone shouts. "She can come work in my room. I'll learn her a thing or two."

"Now, now, boys, this one's with Mr. Thomas," gap-tooth says. "You remember him? Was here about a year ago?"

"That union rep fellow?" someone shouts. "Fuck him. What's he done for us?"

Amanda backs away slowly.

"'S okay, lady. They's just funning ya. They surely are."

Back behind her, in the main room, a huge machine whirs to life. Someone up top must have reengaged the huge steam engine, and its power has been transferred to a conveyor system that lifts the ore up the main shaft. The sound fills the entire mine, like a steady heartbeat.

Someone takes the mule and leads the beast toward a group of carts. Amanda stops stroking the animal and finds herself standing in front of a group of wide-eyed men. Some of them step toward her. The comments come quickly from sharp tongues.

"You like soothing wild beasts there, dearie?"

"What you got them men's clothes on for?"

"You wearing men's underwear too?"

"Why don't you show us how you take care of your union man, hey, girl?"

Amanda turns and runs back up the tunnel, laughter echoing behind her.

"Aw, come back!" someone shouts, his voice barely audible above the conveyor's roar. "We ain't even seen your teats yet!"

Back in the big room, she runs to Jeb, while also eyeing the edges of the huge conveyor system as it swirls around them. The whole thing seems like an earthly beast that could eat men and spit bones without giving the process a second thought.

"Well, that's the lot of it then," Tony says, his conversation with Jeb continuing as if she had never left. "We just take it. Not much you can do, I'd say."

"Damn it, Tony," Jeb says in disgust, barely noticing as Amanda takes his arm. "You've got to try it my way. Maybe you don't want to do a labor rally right now, but I'm telling you, if you don't stand now, it's going to get worse and worse. You've got to call their bluff. It will work. I know it will."

A group of men appears from up Main Street. They carry picks and shovels and draw closer to Tony as he speaks.

"I said I ain't going to risk it. I ain't going to have these men out of a job. I just ain't! We're one of the few mines that ain't got Chinamen working in here yet. It's going to stay that way, far as I'm concerned."

Amanda suddenly realizes that the men who have wandered into the big room are standing in two distinct groups. Instead of looking at Jeb or Tony, the groups seem to be eyeing each other.

One of them motions toward Jeb. "He telling you to strike?"

"We ain't got that far yet," Tony lies.

"Well, anyone says to do it, I'm for it. I can't take another damn wage cut. Barely making it as it is."

"To hell with that!" someone from the other group shouts. "We'll all be out of here if we strike. What then? No, we ain't striking."

Others shout back and forth, either for or against the idea. There's no clear middle ground.

"I said listen to him."

"Who, this union shill?"

"Just listen."

"No. I say don't. Get him the fuck out of here, agitator!"

The word exchange heats up until one of the men steps forward and punches someone in the rival group square in the nose. The man staggers backwards, then falls on his rump.

The battle enjoined, the men start swinging at each other with their tools. But it's halfhearted. These men have been friends and coworkers up until now. Their disagreement is strong, but so is their camaraderie. There's pushing and swearing and jockeying for position, but there's no more punching and no one brings their pickax down on another's head.

One of the men from the group that doesn't want to strike starts to go after Jeb. But his way is blocked by Tony.

Fearless, Jeb jumps onto a small ledge and whistles loudly. The argument stops for a moment. Amanda sees something feral in Jeb's eyes. It's like he's reached into himself and tapped into some basic instinct that she hasn't seen before. But she can tell he's excited by the challenge. He's in his element here.

"Look, some of you know me," Jeb shouts, "and some of you don't. But you all know Tony, and I think you have respect for him, no?"

There are a few nods and a few grumbles.

"Well, whether he wants to strike or not, Tony's been talking to me because he knows there's a big problem here. Hell, you all know it. I'm here to try to help, but it's not going to come easy. In fact, it's going to be tough. I'm telling you that you're going to have to fight for what you want."

"What I want is for the damn Chinamen and Irish to get the hell out of Montana!"

"Fuck off, Billy," replies one of the men, who clearly sounds Irish.

"Yeah, well, we was here first. They're the problem in this town. Not us."

Jeb holds up his hands, pleading for quiet. "The problem, I'm afraid, is the owners of this mine. It's not other workers. It's the management that's squeezing you dry, even while they ship more and more copper out of here. They're willing to toss you aside because someone else is willing to work cheaper. Your beef isn't with the poor bums who are willing to work. We're all willing, right? You need to focus on the management. That's the only enemy right now." And with that, Jeb starts listing some grievances, and what it will mean to the workers if management agrees to address the issues.

His speech goes on for several minutes until his voice grows hoarse from shouting above the din of the machinery.

The two groups of workers finally agree that Jeb will accompany Tony to a meeting with the mine managers. They won't talk about a strike. Not yet. Their approach will be reasonable and measured, focusing on the skills of the current workforce and the challenge of supervising a new crew of unskilled workers who may not speak English.

"We'll appeal to their business sense. They've already made an investment in you men. You know what you're doing. They lose you, and it will take a long time for production to get back up to where it is right now."

Jeb looks around at the doubtful eyes staring back at him.

"That's where we're starting the conversation. If anything more than that happens, you'll hear it directly from Tony. Okay?"

The men grumble, then eventually go back to work, some still eyeing each other suspiciously.

"Good job calming them down," Tony says. "That little conflict has been brewing all week. Now you see what I'm up against."

"I think it's best that we get out of here," Jeb says to Amanda.

Tony escorts them toward the shaft. "Thanks for coming. I'll tell the union you're definitely earning your money here."

"We'll work it out," Jeb says as he looks up, trying to figure out the best way back to the surface. "We always do, right?"

"You want to crank yourself back up in that escape cage?" Tony asks.

"Not if I can avoid it."

Tony nods and pulls a cord that hangs over his head. With a hiss, the big conveyor belt stops. It has waist-deep buckets spaced about four feet apart. Usually ore is loaded into these buckets and hauled vertically up to the surface. But men can stand in the buckets too. He motions for Jeb and Amanda to climb in. By holding tight to each other, they can both fit in a single bucket.

"Keep your arms in, or you'll lose 'em!" Tony says. He shouts something into a pipe that hangs down from the ceiling then pulls the cord again. There's a grinding clank. The bucket accelerates quickly until they find themselves racing upwards, at about three times the speed of their descent. Sliding up past grease-splattered rock, they emerge again into the topside barn. A man at the top pulls a lever, and the conveyor stops with a jerk. If he hadn't stopped their motion, they could have been catapulted over the top of the conveyor where it loops back down and likely thrown into the ore pile that stood a few feet beyond.

"I can see why you didn't want me to come," Amanda says as they climb out.

"Well, at least now you can see what a typical day at the office is like for me." He tries to smile at her, but she can tell he's a bit shaken.

The ride home is little more than a blur to Amanda. Her thoughts are elsewhere, and for some reason, she can't stop thinking about the mules.

Chapter 16

Currents & Connections

It's been a long time since Victor Marius has whistled. The sound surprises him when it forms on his lips and moves out to fill the nearly empty room. The brick walls on all sides of his new lab help give the tune a deep, thrilling resonance.

The tune he whistles is an older song titled "Aura Lee." It's something he heard coming from a player piano within the last week. He's never been much of a singer. But whistling? Well, that's something he does fairly well. But it only happens when he's in the right mood.

Victor continues to whistle as he uses a pile of scrap wood to construct a long lab table. Then he unpacks some boxes—mostly batteries, wires, and terminals given to him by Professor Alton. There's also a rack of test tubes.

Then he turns his efforts toward cleaning—sweeping, wiping windows, hauling out trash. He works for hours and barely notices the labor, happy just to have short-term goals and a long-term purpose.

For two days in a row, sun-up to sundown, he continues the work. When the sun finally sets on the evening of July 30, lights shine inside the lab. Victor has managed to get one of his generators running. He strings wires throughout the room and hangs a variety of bulbs from the ceiling. The equipment was free. Battered old test machines. There are certain advantages to working for the electric company.

Lights in place, he finally gets down to business. Stringing two fat wires the length of the bench, he hooks their frayed ends to a pair of threaded posts. Then he places a small rod on one of the posts and attaches a rudimentary metal disc to the top. To the other post, he attaches a thin, flexible rod and a steel ball.

In the center of the disc, he places a coil that sits on a rotating spindle. The coil has a small copper nub sticking out from one side. It's one of about ten different designs he intends to test. With the right adjustments, a series of sparks will leap across the distance between the disk and the spindle as it spins. His hope is that it will serve as a very rudimentary transmitter that he can adjust to produce evenly timed signals.

"Oh, how I wish I had better tools," he mutters.

His equipment on the *Gossamer* had been much more refined—the result of several experiments he had conducted and retooled.

I'm starting over, he thinks. *Repeating work that I've already done. That's maddening.* Yet he retains a certain excitement, and a hope of doing things even better this time.

About several feet away, he sets up another piece of equipment, also given to him by the professor. It's little more than a two-by-two-foot piece of metal screen, similar to what's found in the window of a home. There are extra wires attached around its perimeter, plus another coil at its bottom. The wires lead to a battery at its base. The rig includes a small box with a dial and a tiny gauge.

When everything is in place, Victor walks to the end of his workbench and throws a switch. A low hum fills the room.

Then he walks over to the screen, squatting to look at it. The idea is that the sparks will produce basic radio waves, and the screen will serve as a rudimentary receiver. He checks the small gauge and sees nothing. He slowly twists the dial back and forth over its full range. Still nothing.

Calmly, steadily, he walks back and forth several times between the transmitter and the receiver. He alternates his adjustments, moving the lever a bit to change the spark pattern, and moving the screen a bit to change the angle of reception. Eventually he sees the tiniest hint of movement in the dial. A smile creeps to his lips.

Did he imagine it?

With a few more adjustments, he manages to increase the gauge's movement by just a hair.

Victor smiles. "You son of a bitch. There you are! I knew it!"

The dial moves no more than the width of two human hairs. To an untrained eye, it looks like little more than a vibration. But the movement is perfectly matched to the *tick tick* of the spark across the room.

Victor raises his arms and twirls in a circle. "That's it! That's it! Back to where I was several months ago. Back when they told me that radio waves don't exist! I proved it then, and I've done it again!"

He punches the air.

Yet his work is far from done. The spark and the detection of its associated wave means little. It's the eventual refinement of the blip—making it longer or shorter, and maybe even being able to adjust frequency or amplitude—that will make all the difference in the world. Only then can a radio wave be used to convey messages.

He has a lot of catching up to do.

Back at the workbench, Victor increases the power to the spark. The ticking sound increases dramatically. Victor's on his way back to look at the receiver when the transmitter suddenly clicks much louder. There's a growing buzz, and suddenly a bolt of pure electrical energy arcs out toward the metal edge of the workbench. Victor feels the hair on his head stand on end as he races toward a shut-off switch. The bolt of white misses him, landing instead on the metal vice attached to the other end of the workbench.

In the few seconds it takes him to turn off the power, the edge of the workbench has already burst into flames. Victor grabs a rag and runs over to beat out the flames. As he does so, the power to the whole room clicks off. He's overloaded the generator.

"God damn it!"

The emergency passes quickly, but the bitter smoke hangs heavy in the room.

Victor mutters to himself as he grabs a wrecking bar and pries open two windows that have been long since painted shut.

Okay, he thinks to himself as the air slowly clears, *so boosting the power to the spark may not be the best way to increase the signal. Or maybe I just need to rework the transmitter design.*

He runs his hands through his hair. *I don't know. I just don't know.*

After cleaning up and getting the lights working again, Victor thinks about bedding down for the night. But there's a loud knock on the huge oak front door.

"Who is it?"

"Hey, you in there, college boy?" A husky voice calls from outside.

Victor laughs and throws open the door. On the doorstep stands Jimmy and Lucas, coming to pay him a visit from Mariner's House. They've obviously been drinking and are not looking to head home yet.

"Yeah, college boy is in here all right. Like my new place? This is what passes for home these days."

He invites them in and they look around, offering their own low whistles.

"It's not much," Victor says. "But I kind of like it."

"Like hell it ain't much," Lucas argues. "Look at the space you got here! And you have electric lights. Blow me down!"

"They don't always work, but yeah, I have 'em."

Jimmy grins and produces a half bottle of whiskey.

"No, no, can't do that. I don't need any more hangovers with you two," Victor warns.

"Oh, for fuck sake, it's just a little christening for your new place!" Jimmy insists. "And it's a going-away party. We're both shipping out in two days."

"What? To where?"

"We both got jobs on a local freighter. Runs a triangle. Here to Brazil, mostly carrying furniture and factory machinery. Then Brazil to Liverpool, mostly with exotic woods and some fruit and shit. Then back home, carrying all sorts of stuff from England. Machinery, casks of gin, clothes, whatever they can haul."

Victor shakes his head. "I thought you guys were retiring soon. Going to get real jobs, you said."

"You got a real job for me?" Lucas asks.

"Well, I might. Maybe in about three weeks. We're going to be stringing more lines. Adding more crew."

"Tell you what then, college boy, we'll come back and talk to you after our first trip. I like the idea of being a landlubber maybe. But men have to make a living in the meantime, ya know?"

Jimmy finds some chipped glasses in Victor's makeshift kitchen area. The whiskey is surprisingly smooth for a cheap brand. By the second glass, they all sit on wooden crates or bags of coal, feet propped up on sawhorses.

Victor is surprised at how easily he slides into a drinking and talking mode. It's like alcohol has become a part of who he is now. After avoiding drinking for so many years, he's strangely discovered that he enjoys it—at least the social side of it.

The light dizziness that he gets from the drink is just a pleasant by-product.

"So what's your plan for this place?" Lucas asks. "You said you wanted to do some kind of experiments. What is it that you're going to do? Build a better light bulb?"

Victor points to the transmitter and receiver and tells them what he's done so far. Then he tries to explain the nature of radio waves, which is tough when he's talking to a couple of guys who are already a few drinks ahead of him.

He decides to pick up one of the softer pieces of cheap coal and draw some sketches on the wall. After several minutes, he senses that the pair has become bored with the lecture, so he cuts it short.

"Let's just say that I need to understand more about how radio waves are produced, how they move through the air, and how they can be detected," he explains. "And this is the space I'll use to do it. After that, I'll start testing again to see how far they can reach."

Jimmy pours himself another glass. A big one.

"I have to tell you, Victor," he says, "I admire someone who can switch gears like you have, and do it successfully. I never had that talent."

He looks around the room. "I mean … look at this place. I've never owned a house or a building in my life. But you? You get wiped out. You come home, and you relaunch. You find yourself a decent job, you buy a place. Hell, you even have electric lights."

Victor deflects the admiration. "Oh, come on. I have a pretty shitty life at the moment."

"Shitty to who? I'd say you're doing just fine. You got something again for yourself. You need to be proud of that, damn it!"

"Shitty enough so that another friend of mine, Thurman, has talked me into a cockamamie scheme to try to box with people while my fists are wired with electricity. How stupid is that?"

Jimmy cracks up. Then wipes his eyes and replies, "You have to tell me when that happens. There's no way I'm going to miss that spectacle.

When the laughter stops, they all take a sip of whiskey.

"Yeah," Victor eventually admits. "You know what? I guess I am proud of where I am, shitty as that is. It beats where I was. I think dreaming of having a new place like this is what's kept me going."

It's nearly midnight when Jimmy and Lucas prepare to leave. They say their good-byes, with Victor wishing them all the best for their upcoming voyage.

"So should we check in with you when we get back?" Lucas asks. "You going to get us real jobs like you said?"

"Maybe I will. Think you two can give up traveling?"

"I don't know. Maybe," says Jimmy. "Have you been able to?"

"Well, not so much on the water anymore. But last weekend, I went to New York to see an old friend and mentor."

As the pair leaves, Victor calls after them.

"Fellas? Thanks for coming by. I mean it. Seems like I always just get lost in my work. It's good to see some familiar faces now and then. I need that."

Chapter 17

New Muscle

Two evenings each week, Irene meets with Devlin and identifies a potential mark. The method for their collusion remains consistent. An unfamiliar face appears in the house, often with a story of a successful business trip. A little flash of cash or a noticeable item of value carried by the man. Things are noticed. Whispers are exchanged.

Devlin is never seen by the victim. At least not until the last possible second. Information is exchanged well away from the parlor. The trick is to make sure his interception of the mark is in no way tied back to Irene.

But when Devlin follows, it's not always easy for him to isolate the mark. It can be a challenge to find a quiet place where he can do his business. Yet, most of the time he's successful. In fact, the South Carolinian has become quite adept in his timing, finding just the right private, mostly hidden spot to approach each of his targets. When the time is right, he stops each one, intimidates them, takes what he can, and departs quickly.

Usually he does not need to display much more than an attitude and a weapon. Sometimes he needs to add a bit of a shove and a threat to show he means business.

This night, Devlin's become a bit greedy. The first man Irene identified turned out to be a total pushover. A dinnerware salesman from central Pennsylvania, the man had plenty of money to burn during his visit to the parlor. Devlin had followed him, then hurried up the other side of the street to get ahead of him. When Devlin popped out from behind a tree, the cowering salesman surrendered his wallet and jewelry too, without any fuss at all. Then he meekly walked away.

An hour later, Devlin is chasing a new mark, and things go smoothly at first. The story, according to one of the girls, is this guy owns a hardware factory. Makes mostly door hinges, knobs and brackets. Looks to be about the same age as Devlin, give or take a couple years.

He apparently said he's a veteran and that he came to Boston to talk with a patent attorney.

It was his cufflinks that caught Irene's attention. Gold, front and back, each with an embedded ruby.

Devlin catches up to his query in roughly the same place as the last mark, and he quickly grabs and slams him up against a wall. But the man doesn't give up his treasures easily. They exchange blows and Devlin ends up with bruised knuckles and a cut lip before he walks away with his prize. Maybe he should have brought one of the guns he's managed to steal over the past few weeks. It would have been far less risky than this hand-to-hand fighting. But it feels good to have won. Especially against a former Union soldier.

He leaves the hardware man on the ground, beaten and bruised, with a dark ribbon of blood running from his nose.

Devlin is around the corner when he hears the man call out to someone, and soon he hears a rush of footsteps. There are at least four other men heading his way. He knows enough not to run. The sound of his footsteps will give him away. Instead, he fades into a narrow carriageway between buildings, slips his shoes off, and heads out the far side, clinging to shadows along the way. Then he doubles back to Irene's place. He makes sure to come in through the rear door, so no one sees his bloody lip.

Back at the scene of the mugging, four men crowd around their friend. "Who was it, Henry? Who did this?"

The victim has trouble standing. He rests on all fours on the cobblestones, coughing blood and spitting out a tooth.

"Fucking bastard. I'll kill 'em! I'll shoot him right between his shitty little eyes."

"I'm with you, Albert. You still carrying that snubbed-off Remington? The one you had at Shiloh?"

"Goddamn right, I do. Always carry it. Never had a chance to pull it out." He looks the other men in the eyes. "You carrying too?"

Nods all around.

The victim, Henry, lifts a shaking hand. Points in the direction where Devlin disappeared. Two of the men run ahead, but slow down when they see nothing.

In a garbled voice, Henry tries to explain. "Pretty sure he was waiting for me. He was no street thief, that one. Working with someone. Must have known I was going to be walking here. I'm very sure of that."

"Where were you before this?" Albert asks. But Henry shakes his head and looks away.

"Jesus Christ, Hen. All the drinking and whoring we did in Tennessee? And you're going to clam up on us now? I don't care if you're some bigshot businessman now. We're here for our reunion You think any of us give a damn if you stopped to dip your winky along the way? You need to tell us what the fuck happened.

Henry eventually catches his breath, and talks about the house where he stopped. "The man who robbed me... he had a southern accent. Mid-40s. Bastard knew how to fight too. We've all saw the likes of him before."

"Son of a bitch. Don't know why we didn't just kill them all."

"So tell us about this house," Albert insists.

Henry takes a deep breath.

"Pretty woman, thin, she runs the place. Darleen or Irene or something like that. Only talked to her briefly. Nothing goes on there that she doesn't know about."

Henry gives them rough directions, then adds, "Just follow the music."

One of the men, Roy, stays with Henry. The other three set out to find the house.

"And get my damn cufflinks back," Henry calls after them. "My wife gave those to me!"

It doesn't take them long to hear the music and to find their way to the front door. Once inside, they're all business, walking in unison toward the back bar. Conversations stop and all eyes are on them.

Albert, the largest of the group, nods to the bartender, picks up a glass and throws it against the back bar, breaking two bottles. The music stops too. The bartender starts to object but finds the barrel of a snub-nose Remington pressed up against the bridge of his nose.

"Now you listen to me, and you listen good," Albert says in a cool tone. You tell the madam of this house to get her skinny ass down here right now, 'else there's going to be more things busted up than just some bottles."

The bartender says nothing. But his eyes tell all. He looks toward the stairs, sliding upward to where a shadow can be seen next to the top of the bannister.

Chapter 18

Extension

The ride back from the copper mine is a quiet one. Jeb is lost in thought, and Amanda isn't sure what to think about seeing a fight nearly erupt. Nor does she know what to think of the rough men who might have taken advantage of her with no thread of civility to govern their lust. Her contemplation drifts back and forth between anger at their male belligerence, and disappointment in herself at not being more assertive and challenging in the face of their threats.

Mostly she wonders if her five feet three inches of spunk and grit would have been enough to fight them off, had it come to that.

Jeb's voice finally breaks the silence. "You know how I said we'd head out for San Francisco in about a week?"

She nods.

"Well, now I'm thinking it may take a bit longer than that."

She raises her eyebrows and tips her head a bit. "Longer? Why?"

"Well, there's more trouble here than I bargained for. We need a new strategy. This is going to take some doing."

Amanda tries not to let her disappointment show, but it's obvious that she doesn't like this place. Originally she and Jeb had planned to be here just four days.

"I thought you had a job waiting for you in California."

"I do. Sort of. The job doesn't really start until I get there. So we have time."

She nods slowly. "Okay. So … how much longer do you think?"

"I don't know. Another week. Maybe two."

It's not the answer Amanda hopes to hear. She sits silently for over a minute. Jeb finally starts talking, just to fill the silence.

"Look, I know this is a rough place for a woman. Half the girls in town are whores, and the other half are rich women married to the mine executives. There's no middle ground at all. Certainly no one like you. But there are some pockets of civility here and there. I think you'll see that."

More silence.

"How about if I take you to … um … a show tomorrow night? Yeah, there we go. Does that sound good?"

Amanda sighs. "I suppose if we're going to be here a while, I should try to make the best of it. Yes, a show sounds nice. I suppose it's dancing girls? Some sort of tawdry follies? What else could we expect here?"

"Something like that. But not as bad as you make it sound. There's a place in town where they have a stage surrounded by tables. I hear there's a traveling cabaret group there with a pretty wild show. They have women who can walk on the ceiling!"

Amanda shakes her head. "I don't believe that for a minute. The ceiling? How on earth would they do that? Ropes?"

"I don't rightly know," Jeb replies, his voice mimicking one of the salty old minors. "I just hear-tell that they can do it, and I wants to see it for myself."

"You 'hear tell,' hmm?"

"Yes, indeedy!"

"Well, that sort of talk is one thing I'm *not* going to miss, if and when we get out of here," she says as their wagon pulls back into town. "I actually miss the East Coast way of speaking."

Chapter 19

Moving

One hand pressed against her breastbone and the other leaning against the top stair post, Irene listens to the voices as they drift up from below. Behind her, Devlin waits in the doorway of the bedroom. After he doubled back to the house, he came in the back door and slipped up the rear staircase. He told Irene everything about the robbery, and that he might have been followed. Neither thought that he would be tracked down so quickly.

It would have been much easier if the wronged parties had called the police. Police officers – Irene could deal with. But this crew, they seem wilder, angrier and far less predictable. Devlin stays behind her, but he paces. He's ready to do what he needs to do. Ready for a fight.

Irene waves him off.

"You just stay quiet, dear. We've dealt with these issues before. Best that you aren't seen at all." She urges him to head back to the rear exit. Reluctantly, he does so. But he has no intention of leaving her unprotected. She turns to walk down the stairs. Before he leaves, Devlin grabs those weapons he had left behind, a sawed-off shotgun and a black nickel derringer.

As Irene descends the main staircase, Devlin slips back down the rear stairs and heads outside. Circling around to the front door, he can see there's no waiting there. The men making the commotion are all inside. Other customers watch in silence. Devlin realizes the men who are looking

130

for him don't really know what he looks likes, so he slips into the parlor and quietly sits at one of the far tables.

"May I ask you gentlemen what the problem is?" Irene asks as she reaches the bottom of the stairs. Then she elegantly glides into the room, and Albert turns to see her. He gestures with his gun. "A friend of ours paid you a visit earlier tonight," he explains. "Had a bit of a run-in with a ruffian on his way home. It's pretty obvious that he was followed from here."

Irene stands straight and tall. "I'm sorry to hear that. We run a very nice place here. Discrete and fun for all. I certainly don't like to hear about any of my clients having problems."

"That a fact?"

"It very much is, sir. And we didn't have anything to do with, well, whatever happened after he left. So, I'll ask you to put your gun down and leave my establishment immediately."

He grits his teeth. "No can do, Madam. See, it's pretty obvious to me that whoever followed him came right from here. And they had information that obviously came from one of your girls. Our friend was targeted."

"That's nonsense."

Albert turns and fires a bullet into the back bar, shattering another bottle, dark rum this time, and chipping the mirror behind it. Devlin's hand slips into his coat. He grasps the handle of the sawed-off, but stays still for the moment.

"That enough nonsense for you?" Albert demands. "Now I'll give you one minute to bring my friend's money out to me. Also his cufflinks. Bring everything right down here, and we'll call it a day. But I also want the name of the man who did it. Understand? Do we have an issue with any of this?"

The bartender moves slightly and finds the gun pointed at the center of his face once again.

"You know what?" Albert shouts, "It's been a while since I've done any killing. Over 25 years in fact. Don't mind doing it again if I have to." He looks the crowd over, then steps up the volume of his voice. "The man who robbed my friend had a southern accent. Big man. Knew his business. Based on his age, I'd say it's more than likely he was a goddamn rebel back in the day. That the kind of vermin you want to keep company with here? Humm? Do any of you know such a man?"

Devlin has been around the house long enough that a few people in the room know him. He feels their eyes on him, but no one says a word. And so far, the interloper has not noticed the direction of their gazes.

Irene steps forward again to urge calm. Albert backhands her hard, hitting her cheek and sending her falling backward to the carpet. He points his gun directly down at her.

Devlin starts to rise.

Back during the war, fights were not always as heroic as veterans like to recall. The stories they tell years later don't

132

always capture the real essence of battle. There's a lot of bluffing. A lot of men don't really want to kill if they don't have to. It's easier for all if they can just get their enemy to turn and run. So sometimes soldiers simply shoot over the other troop's heads, trying to scare them off. Sometimes they just shoot one of the enemy in the leg and scream "now git" to the others.

Sometimes the others do git. And that's the end of the battle.

But when no one backs down, and when things do come to a head, it's time to move. That's what Devlin's squad used to call it. Others did too.

Let's move on them.

Everyone knew what that meant. All bluffing was done. It meant that it was time to move in for the kill. It meant it was time to do the very thing that soldiers were trained to do, and usually it was quick and brutal.

As Albert points the gun down directly at Irene, he slowly cocks it. Devlin knows it's time to move. There will be no bluffing now, and no negotiations.

Coat swinging open as he steps from the table, Devlin slides the sawed-off up and out of his long inner pocket. He pulls it upward. The handle sits smooth and warm in his hand.

Albert senses the movement and turns, but Devlin's approach is fast and direct. He pumps a round of heavy birdshot directly into the old Union soldier's left side, and it feels good, to Devlin, to do so. An old battle rejoined. No blue uniform to shoot at, this time, but his enemy's attitude is deeply federal. Devlin always has hated that attitude. He squints as he cuts the man down.

Albert bucks with the hit, stumbles sideways and falls. The crowd in the parlor rushes toward the exits. Devlin tells Irene to stay down.

The men who came with Albert already have their guns drawn, prompting Devlin to move sideways. In this tight space, it's tough to swing a gun and target a moving man. Devlin pumps another round, but because he is moving, he doesn't aim carefully enough. The birdshot barely grazes his target's coat.

Bullets fly now, but he manages to stay ahead of them. He runs toward the men, to their left side, causing them to try to aim their guns as they swing them across their own chests. It's an old trick that makes it very hard for them to draw a bead. Devlin spins and swings the shotgun waist high, and lets rip with another blast. This one catches one of the men in the hip. As the man falls, he fires once directly toward Devlin and once high, hitting nothing but the ceiling. Devlin throws a table on its side and dives behind it. Somehow he wasn't hit. But the shotgun won't cock again. He realizes the first bullet hit the gun right in the side of the pump action. It's useless now. He casts it aside and pulls out his derringer.

There's silence for a moment. He can't see the remaining man, but knows he's nearby. The old soldier isn't going to retreat. Devlin hears a step. Then another. Hears the gun fire at the heavy table. The oak splinters but the round doesn't penetrate. The sound is enough to let Devlin know where the shooter stands. He places his foot against the table and gives it a mighty shove. It hits his opponent square in the legs, causing him to stumble back. Devlin quickly fires up at him, striking him in the chest.

The man just stands there looking at Devlin. It's a long moment. Then he drags his fingers along his chest. That chest makes a low sucking sound when the man tries to breathe. His fingers are bloody. Closing his eyes, he falls forward, and just like that, the battle is over. At least for now.

"Get out!" Irene shouts to him. "Get out now before the police come."

"Are you okay?"

"Yes. I'm fine. Shaken, but fine."

"Are they dead?" he demands. "I don't think they all can be dead. It's just bird…"

"It doesn't matter," she insists.

"But it does," Devlin replies. "We need to erase this. We want no eyes left from the hunted, Irene!"

He quickly reloads and walks to look at the victims. The man he shot in the chest looks dead, but he can't be sure. The other two are still alive, look up at him, fear and anger in their eyes. He points his weapon downward at the first man.

"Dev! No!" Irene screams.

She runs to him, tugging at his arm.

"Stop it!" he yells. But he doesn't fight her grasp. He steps back. Looks at one of the men, who is stirring and groaning. "These were the boys in blue, Irene! All of them… they are still my enemy. They always will be."

She shakes her head no.

"He struck you. Knocked you down. Was ready to put a bullet into you. Don't you think for a minute that they won't come after you again if we let them live!"

"She drags him by his arm to a quiet corner behind a curtain. You need to leave, Devlin. You need to run. Few people know you here. No one got a good look at you. I'll just tell them that I don't know who you are."

"That won't work. They came here looking for both of us!"

"Just… just go!" she pushes him toward the back door.

"I'll send for you when I can. I'll write a note."

"Don't sign your real name."

"Of course, I won't. I'll just sign it… I'll say… 'right and proper.' Okay? You'll know who it's from."

He kisses her then quickly disappears. Out into the night. Worried for her and about what just happened. Worried for himself. Worried about who might track him down.

What he should do is leave Boston. Immediately. But there's too much at stake. He doesn't want to leave the puzzle box behind. He knows that's foolish, given that he's not even certain what's inside.

But, just maybe, he doesn't want to leave Irene either.

Chapter 20

Recovery

Raindrops begin to fall on the front bay window of Jonathan Morgan's home. They prompt him to rush to his front stoop. The afternoon news is due, and if there's anything Jonathan dislikes, it's a soggy paper. He waits under the portico, smoking a commercially rolled Bal Tiga cigarette and nodding casually to neighbors as they hurry past, anxious to get out of the rain.

The paperboy is late. But Jonathan sees another lad rushing up the street, legs pushing hard as he sits in the middle of a high-wheeled tricycle.

"Mr. Morgan? Mr. Jonathan Morgan?"

"Could be, lad. Who wants to know?"

"Message for you, sir."

Morgan eyes the boy suspiciously. He doesn't wear the hat or uniform of a Western Union messenger, nor any other delivery service.

"Who do you work for, lad?"

The boy climbs off his three-wheeled contraption and pushes it back against the curb so it won't roll away. "I live near the police station. They pay me ten cents for every message I deliver. I guess it keeps them from having to send a policeman around. I get maybe three or four messages to deliver every morning."

The old man nods and holds out his hand, cigarette still lit, to receive the envelope. The lad stands by while he opens it, obviously waiting for a tip. *Quite the young entrepreneur, isn't he,* Jonathan thinks, *playing both sides of the delivery to get a little coin.* Morgan grumbles, hands the lad a nickel, and waves him off.

The rain starts to fall in earnest as the messenger climbs back onto his wicker seat. Jonathan reads the note. It's handwritten, dashed off in a hurry by a policeman who obviously has had very little training in proper penmanship. But the news is welcome.

Dear Mr. Morgan.

I believe we may have located a piece of property that was stolen from your home. It's a small wooden box, fitting the exact description that was given to the police when your home was burglarized over three weeks ago.

If you could stop by the police office that is located within the Boylston Street Fire Station, the duty sergeant can show you the box to see if it is indeed your missing item. We ask that you do this within the next ten days.

Sergeant B. Ludlow

Boston Police

Morgan smiles and tucks the letter into his coat. Suddenly the afternoon paper doesn't matter anymore. Let it get wet.

"Beverly?" he calls out as he rushes back into the house. "Beverly, you won't believe the news! Get your raincoat!"

Chapter 21

Ceiling Walkers

Drop of water, falling from a sweating pitcher.

It tumbles through the humid air on a warm summer evening and lands on the shoe of a harried waiter as he weaves through the crowd.

The waiter works in the pub section of Butte's infamous Dumas Hotel. More drops form and fall as he moves. The rhythm is perfect. A new drop drips on the same shoe every fourth step. When the waiter arrives at Amanda and Jeb's table, it looks as if he's wearing two different shoes, one dull and dark gray, the other slick and shiny like patent leather. Amanda smiles as she looks at his feet.

"When does the show start?" Jeb asks as they accept the one-page menus.

"In about a half hour," the waiter replies, pouring two glasses of water with a practiced flick of his wrist. "That is, as long as they get the stage set. Guess they're still having trouble with it." He nods toward a muffled banging sound behind a heavy curtain.

The couple orders a meal of lamb stew and a light bread known as bread sponge. Jeb asks for a draft beer while Amanda orders a small glass of Catawba. It's the first wine she's had since her night on the porch, waiting for Wayne.

As they pass the time at their table, their conversation is pleasant, if a bit forced. It's nice to get out and see a show, but their unresolved issue about when to leave town hangs between them like a curtain. Butte isn't a place where Amanda wants to remain for more than a few more days. Without a plan or a timetable, she feels adrift.

Yet looking across the table, at the face of this man she may very well love, the current uncertainty feels somewhat tolerable—at least for a while.

Amanda surveys the room, amused at what she sees. Never having set foot inside a house of ill repute before, she's surprised not only by the size of the place, but also by how formal it seems. In many ways, it looks the same as any fancy hotel, right down to the Saturday evening entertainment. But at the periphery, upon closer look, the seedy "other business" of the place is all too apparent.

There are a handful of couples here and there. But most of the tables are occupied by groups of men. They spend as much time looking around the room as they do talking to each other. Other men, obviously laborers and miners who have tried to clean themselves up a bit and put on their best clothes for the evening, don't want to spend the money that's expected at a dining table. They tend to lurk around the room's back walls and doorways, mugs of beer in hand. Meanwhile, over by the bar, about a dozen women wearing fancy dresses and far too much rouge make small talk with those men who are either brave enough or drunk enough to venture into their realm.

In some ways, the whole scene reminds Amanda of the dances and fairs she used to attend on holidays back in Boston. Except that this mating ritual has an underlying sleaziness. She turns to Jeb, a half grin forming on her lips.

"I can't believe you brought me to a bordello, Jeb. I mean … honestly."

"You knew we were coming here."

"Well, at least let me pretend that I'm still a lady!" She bats her eyes.

He chuckles. "Hey, you said you wanted to see this show, right? When I bought tickets, I thought they were going to perform in a tent, but this is where they ended up setting up."

"Why do you think they switched the show to here?"

"The people who run this place are shrewd business folk. They don't want any competition in town that might take their crowd away. Best to cut a deal and get them to perform inside, I guess. They probably just promised them food, drinks, and beds for the night. Something like that looks mighty attractive to a traveling troupe."

Amanda feigns disdain. But she forces the smile from her face. "You know what's funny? I don't even care where we are. A couple months ago, I'd have been mortified to even set foot in a place like this. I was a married woman. A church-going woman. I baked pies and entered them in the county fair. I thought places like this were dens of sin and debauchery."

"Well, they are, aren't they?"

"Yes, I suppose. But the difference is, I really don't care now. It's funny how one develops a 'live-and-let-live' philosophy when one's own life has grown disorderly and chaotic. Any one of us could end up in a place like this, given the right circumstances."

Amanda points toward the disheveled miners by the far wall. "I used to look at men like that and think of them as wicked and shameful. Why can't they look and act like respectable gentlemen? Now I mostly just see lonely human beings who are trying their best to survive. I see men who are looking to make some kind of human connection that might keep them going."

Jeb seems unsure what to say. He's been too close to places like this, for too long, to think of this as anything other than the way life is. "You know, Amanda," he stumbles for words, "there's over 23,000 people in Butte. And you'll find enough crime and corruption here for a city three times its size. Meanwhile, there's only enough women here for a city less than half this size. That makes for a pretty volatile mix. So, you either learn to connive and thrive in a place like this, or you get out. I'm willing to bet that very few of those men over there will still be in town three years from now. They'll make a little money and move on. But you can bet there's always going to be a new supply of desperate men who will drift in to take their place. The mine owners count on that. And that makes a place like this all the rougher."

Their meal arrives, carried by the waiter with one wet shoe. They eat ravenously and finish up just as the gaslights dim and a woman in a green velvet dress steps onto the stage.

"Is that the madam of the house?" Amanda whispers.

"Not really. She's in charge of the pub area, and she arranges the musical entertainment. The madam in charge of the … umm … more personal entertainment works out of a backroom. If you see her in here at all, she'll be sitting near that little alcove at the far end of the bar."

With a soft drumroll, the festivities start.

"Ladies and gentlemen!" the woman in velvet calls out. "I thank you for your patience, and I promise you that patience will be rewarded. Never in the history of this state has there been a production to rival this one!" Her broad, sweeping gestures, formal tone, and elegant style hint that she's had some East Coast theater training.

"Tonight, straight from their five-week sold-out run in Denver, we welcome the Amazing Zimbani Girls!" Hands outstretched, she waits for the hoots, hollers, and claps to die down. "This marvelous group has toured Europe and the Far East, where they have learned feats of magic and derring-do that no other traveling shows have been able to accomplish. You will see dancing, you will see acrobatics and magic, and you will see feats that defy the very laws of physics!"

With a practiced sweep of her hand, the woman in green gestures to a tall red velvet curtain as it starts to open. "And now, ladies and gentlemen, the Dumas Hotel presents … The Amazing Zimbani Girls!"

A piano starts playing in the new syncopated style that's become popular in the larger cities. Eight girls, wearing the shortest skirts Amanda has ever seen, start to dance across the stage with linked arms. They kick high and smile broadly. Their dancing is not highly polished. Their timing is off, and some of the women kick noticeably higher than the others, but the crowd barely notices. Men whoop and call and whistle. They appreciate the women for what they are—women who are willing to show a little leg.

The show goes on for nearly forty-five minutes. Girls do song and dance numbers in groups of threes and fours. Outfits get slightly skimpier. One of the women juggles while the others change costumes. They return on small scooters, pushing themselves along, with broad red-lipstick smiles, long scarves flying behind them as they spin about the stage. Each scarf is a different bright color, and Amanda, despite her amusement at the rough feel of the production, finds herself caught up in the beauty of it. The women may not be top-quality performers, but they seem to enjoy what they do, and they draw everyone in.

Four of the women wheel themselves to center stage to sing a bawdy song while the others roll off. When the song ends, the other four return, wearing outfits that look more appropriate for a sports team than a dance troop. The reason for the loose, skimpy clothing becomes apparent as one of the girls lies flat and then is hoisted above the others. Small, curved spikes are visible on the bottom of her shoes.

Holding her high, they move her toward one of the walls until her feet touch. She twists her feet a bit until they click into place.

It's then that Amanda and Jeb, whispering to each other, realize that the wall is actually a large pegboard. The girl has curved spikes on the bottom of her feet that stick into the peg holes. Those who support the girl let go one by one until she is supported at her shoulders by just one woman's hand reaching up from below. It obviously takes great effort for her to remain rigid.

The crowd starts clapping in time with the piano music. The woman turns sideways to better distribute her weight and starts an awkward shuffle. At first, she walks horizontally, with a hand from one of the women still supporting her. Her progress is slow. For each step, she has to unhook one foot from tiny holes in the wall, extend it forward, and then wiggle it to hook it back into the wall again. The supporting hand presses up under her shoulder. With a wince or two, she walks from the left side of the stage, along the back wall, then onto the right side. Once her circuit is complete, the other women rush over to help her back down. The crowd roars its approval as the woman bows, muscles quivering from the effort.

The trick is repeated by two other women, then the music changes, and they all fall back into their high-kicking pattern again. In their short shorts, a great deal of leg is now visible, and the men whistle and stomp their feet. One of the men shoots his gun in the air, and hotel staffers rush over to give him hell.

By this time, the waiter has cleared Jeb and Amanda's table. Jeb orders another drink, but Amanda declines. She's had enough. She looks around and notices that all the men in the pub are staring intently at the stage. She also notices that some of the women in the bar area look restless. The show is obviously cutting into their trade, and they aren't happy about it.

After the dance number winds down, the piano music suddenly changes. It rises into a very perilous melody, with climbing and descending scales meant to make the hair stand up on the back of one's neck.

The whole audience leans forward. One of the girls is hoisted up high again, this time with her legs pointing toward the top of the wall. She hooks her feet into the wall where it curves toward the ceiling. Using her arms for support, she presses up from the extended hands of the other dancers and slowly walks higher. With about three steps she moves onto the ceiling, then pulls herself up and out of their reach.

She has no other support now than her special shoes.

The piano stops. No one says a word. In dead silence, she slowly walks, one step at a time, across the ceiling, light-brown tresses slipping loose from their combs and hanging down like curly icicles. To keep her hands still she grips a thick belt at her waist. Her baggy shorts fall back, revealing almost her entire leg. The last few steps are obviously hard for her. Her legs shake and seem to want to flop downward each time she unhooks them. But by sheer force of will, and considerable athletic prowess, she gracefully keeps herself suspended. Eventually she reaches the other curve and descends into the waiting arms of the other dancers.

The crowd explodes in a wave of cheering and catcalls as the girls bow and walk off.

Somewhere behind her, Amanda hears a man yell to a friend, "God damn, I bet that one's hell in bed, eh? Wonder if she's taking any visitors while she's here."

"You kidding, Ned?" someone else yells back. "I wager that she'd kill you. Wear you right out like a pack mule."

"Yeah, yeah," Ned responds. "But, damn, what a way to …."

The rest of his comments are lost in the noise. The crowd begins a rhythmic clap and chant, shaking the roof of the place with their applause. They're not going to leave until they see the stunt again.

There's a brief argument near the side door. It looks like the man who shot his gun is being escorted from the building, but not without a lot of swearing and posturing. Amanda tries to hear what he's saying as he points his finger at the managers, but it's far too noisy.

Eventually the curtain reopens, and it's the women again, dancing and kicking like before. Silver dollars and small gold nuggets are tossed onto the stage. One of the women pulls at the neckline of her outfit until her breasts are almost exposed. She winks at the men as they whoop. They yell for more.

Finally, the group falls back into place, lifting the same woman high again, letting her attach her feet to the wall, then pushing her, once again, up and away. She slowly hooks and steps, hooks and steps, moving onto the ceiling.

Things grow quiet again. She looks tired, and her legs shake as she makes her second inverted trip across the top of the stage. The effect is just as dreamlike as before. An upside-down woman, walking on the ceiling just as if she's slowly strolling down the street. Is it real? Is it a trick? Or is it just the alcohol taking hold?

"Leave me the hell alone!"

A deep voice booms out from the doorway. It's the man who was being escorted out. He's obviously inebriated and very angry that he's missing the final act of the show. He grabs at the rusty Colt .45 that was taken from him by one of the hotel managers.

"And give me that."

"You'll get it back when we're outside. Now let's go."

"You think so, huh?" The man strikes the manager and pulls hard at the gun. It discharges as it's ripped from the manager's hands. The bullet hisses over the crowd and strikes the forward part of the ceiling area above the stage. The wood there splinters and flies apart.

The upside-down woman freezes in place, eyes darting around the stage. She's safely away from the bullet, but the ceiling shakes from the impact. There's a low splintering sound as the narrow support at the front of the structure starts to give way. It doesn't droop more than a few inches, but that sagging action shakes the structure, and the inverted woman finds herself swaying. Her scream echoes through the room as the pegs on the bottom of her feet pop loose from the holes. She extends her hands, trying to break her fall, as the rest of the troupe rushes toward her. But she lands with a sickening thud on the stage. Her head takes a good part of the impact.

She lies terribly still on the wooden floor.

The curtain quickly closes, and there are muffled shouts for a doctor backstage.

Screaming and crying can be heard. The woman in the green dress returns to the stage, trying to calm the crowd and urging everyone to leave in an orderly fashion. Several of the women from the bar rush out ahead of the crowd, taking up positions near the front of Venus Alley.

The crowd lingers out front for a while, then starts to dissipate. Amanda looks sick as she and Jeb walk back toward the hotel.

"Think she'll be all right?" Jeb asks, genuinely concerned.

"You know she won't. How could anyone be all right after a fall like that?"

They walk on in silence until Jeb lets out a long sigh. "It's not fair, you know? A group like that, they have no sort of protection at all. You see how tired she looked? Doing the same risky stunt, night after night, and for what? A few dollars? For some admiring looks? If that woman lives, she may end up in a wheelchair. Or maybe she'll be a vegetable, babbling away in some corner. The producers of that show won't help her. They'll just move on. They might send her another paycheck or two, then they're done."

"Isn't that the way things work?" Amanda asks. "Isn't it always that way?"

"No. It's not," Jeb says, his voice showing both anger and inspiration. "At least it doesn't have to be. There can be safety rules. There can be insurance. Union rules and limits. There's lots of different ways a theater troupe can provide protection. Workers just have to insist on it. That's right.

Even lowly actors and acrobats can unionize and insist on protections."

For the first time, Amanda feels like she understands the things that drive Jeb. The danger he faces. The uncertainty. All of it. She's hated the quirks of his career up until now. But finally, she also can see his cause as noble. It takes a brutal example like the falling girl to make people understand such things sometimes, but now she can see it clearly.

Back at the hotel, she rubs Jeb's back, soothing his anger. Eventually they crawl into the softness of the feather mattress and make some of the most intense love either of them has ever felt.

Chapter 22

For Want of a Jug

For some reason, while standing atop his radio tower, Victor Marius looks down at his feet. He's somewhat shocked by the view. The long drop to the ground isn't what surprises him, nor is it his shoes. What catches his eye is his body. He's lost the gaunt thinness that he previously saw in his legs. For the first time since being lost and then found at sea, he feels robust. There is a healthy aspect to his thighs now.

Placing his wrench in his back pocket, he curls his fingers around one of the tower supports and instinctively feels his face with the other. His cheeks, formerly gaunt, now feel thickened.

He's never felt better. He feels strong and alive. His condition has nothing to do with his ordeal at sea. Yet, he's still a bit skinny because on most days he simply forgets to eat. He's so wrapped up in his work that nothing else matters.

My goodness, he thinks to himself, *I'll have to pay more attention.*

Finishing his final adjustment on the tower, Victor climbs down, forces himself to grab a lunch of ham, cheddar cheese, and biscuits, then rushes back to his workbench.

Turning the dial on a transmitter, he broadcasts a simple wideband *blap* of static that repeats every five seconds. Rushing to a receiver at the other end of the room, he tries to pick up the signal until he finally throws down his screwdriver in disgust. He hasn't received a decent signal since his initial success a few days before.

The same icebox that holds his ham and beef jerky also holds a ceramic jug of homemade strawberry wine, compliments of a local farmer's market. It's a bit tart for his preferences, but it's not terrible. He sits on a wooden box and sips directly from the jug. Staring at the receiver, he silently waits for inspiration to come.

Half a jug later, the whole workbench is a blur, and he's come up with no new pieces to arrange in his puzzle. Even the wine can't help him produce a coveted "aha!" moment that will help him continue.

The jug is dry. He heads to the door. The farmer's market will be shutting down soon. Maybe he can find another jug. He's developed quite a taste for it lately.

Somewhere in the back of his mind, he recalls an expression about the acorn not falling far from the tree.

Feeling like he needs another reason besides the wine to make his trip to the nearby crossroads, he decides to also stop into the general store. There's a small Western Union counter in the back.

DEAR NIKOLA, he dictates once he reaches the counter, NEED HELP WITH MY LATEST EXPERIMENTS. [STOP] TRANSMISSIONS FAULTY OR RECEIVER FAULTY. [STOP] NOT SURE WHICH. PHONE CALL POSSIBLE? PLEASE ADVISE. [STOP]

The clerk looks up from his pencil as Victor finishes the dictation. "Send it to Nikola Tesla," Victor tells him, "care of this address ...."

His outreach complete, Victor walks to the nearly deserted market. Sunday is never as busy as Saturday, but some farmers arrive early on both days in order to make their sales. By 2:00 p.m., most are packing what's left of their produce into their carts.

The farmer who sells the homemade wine has four jugs in his wagon. They sit beside a chicken crate that holds just one skinny hen. She wouldn't make much of a meal, but she could probably feed one man.

The farmer nods, recognizing Victor from previous transactions.

"How about if I buy the whole lot from you," he offers, "jugs and the chicken, for three dollars?"

The farmer scratches his stubble, then hooks his thumbs behind his overall straps.

"Three-fifty. Best I can do."

Victor tries not to smirk. He would have gone as high as four. "I live a half mile west. You come to the market from that direction, don't you? I've seen you on the road."

The farmer nods.

"How about we say we have a deal at three-fifty—if you drop everything off at my place and give me a ride too?"

The farmer squints a bit. But it's more for show than for any real objection. "Well, ayah, 'spose we could do that."

The money changes hands, and Victor climbs into the wagon. By the time they round the corner near his home, at least another six ounces of wine is gone. Victor stares out into space, calculating something in his head.

"I'm not demodulating. That's the problem," he says to the floor of the wagon. "At least not the right way. That's why I can't pick up the signal."

"Eh?" the farmer calls over his shoulder.

"Oh, sorry. Some experiments that I'm running." He realizes his words are a bit slurred, and it embarrasses him. Feeling like he needs to explain himself to the farmer, he calls up the metaphor of the telegraph. "I'm in the business of building telegraphs. I mean, it's sort of like that, but a little different." He points up the road to his lab building. "You'll see that I don't live in a house exactly. It's more of a workshop."

The farmer says nothing. He pulls a matchstick out of his pocket and starts to chew.

"I was just thinking out loud, I guess, because I think I've finally figured out a problem."

"Don't bother me none," the farmer says through his teeth. "You're talking to a man who spends his days out in the field. If you don't talk to yourself, sometimes there's no one to talk to at all."

They pull up at Victor's shop and quickly unload the wine and the squawking hen. Victor shakes the man's hand.

"One thing about talking when no one is around," the farmer says as he picks up the leads. "Just talking to yourself is okay. Helps you organize your thoughts. But take it from an old hand. If you start talking to people who aren't there, well, then you've got a problem. That's when you know you've got to get yourself to town a little more often."

He winks and snaps the leads.

Victor looks down at the chicken. The chicken looks directly back at him.

Even though the hen is too small to share, Victor still wishes that Jimmy and Lucas would stop by tonight. Work may be important, but he does enjoy their company.

He walks back to his workbench and bends a tiny piece of wire, making a rudimentary spring, then inserts it at the base of his receiver, right near where the antenna attaches. He works far into the night. Before bed, he takes an injection of his opium and steroid concoction. A wave of pleasure rushes over him, then an immense feeling of being tired. But before falling asleep, he forces himself to do 100 pushups, then 60 lifts of his brass gear barbell. It's all a blissful haze.

Then he falls into bed. As he drifts off, his mind races, not with dreams of antennas, not with dreams of peaceful slumber, but with images of a fight. He dreams of taking on all comers, and letting the knocked-out bodies pile up around him.

Chapter 23

Lingering Days, Lingering Doubts

The next several days are a mixed blessing for Amanda. At times, she and Jeb seem like the best of friends. They eat breakfast and dinner together, laugh together, and sleep together. As Jeb holds his meetings and makes additional trips out to the mines, she busies herself with walks, reading, and trips to the small downtown shops. What she buys is little more than bare necessities. She has but a few dollars left from her working days in Kansas City, and Jeb hasn't received a stipend from any of his union clients in weeks.

As she waits, the days stretch out well past two weeks.

It's an awkward existence. If she knew she was going to be here this long, she could have tried to find work immediately. Or she could have just said no to the idea of staying, and she could have made plans to leave on her own.

That troubling thought always lurks at the back of her mind. Much as she enjoys Jeb, the life he leads remains terribly disconcerting to her. It's tentative. It's chaotic. Plus, there's always a hint of violence lurking in the background. The corruption and constant secret dealings make the whole business seem inherently dishonest.

What's worse, Jeb himself seems like a different man when he's meeting with his business associates. She can't quite put her finger on what it is, but the "business" in which they participate seems to possess a level of ferocity and avarice that erodes the integrity of all participants.

Yet still she waits. She sees enough good in Jeb to keep her here.

More days pass, August unravels toward its humid end, and the tension between them stretches ever tighter.

Jeb returns one evening with a bruise over his left eye. "It's nothing," he says. "Just bumped into a low-hanging beam." But the bruises on his knuckles indicate there's more to the story.

It also troubles her that some of his meetings are held at the Dumas Hotel. "Just business," he says. "You know how it is. Men come from out of town, they're looking to cut loose a bit. We buy them drinks. The women smile at them. It's not a big deal, Amanda. You have to understand that. It's how we move things toward agreement."

And she does try to understand. But the smell of perfume on his shirt makes empathy difficult to sustain. And then there's the telegrams that he exchanges with someone back east. She still hasn't figured out what they're all about.

They exchange harsh words one night when Jeb fails to join her for dinner. There's anger in his eyes and whiskey on his breath as he slams his hand down on the small table in their room.

"Damn it! I said I might be late. You need to understand that, woman. That's just what happens sometimes."

She looks at him like the stranger he's starting to become. "What I understand, Jeb, is that we've become stuck, somehow. You may have business here, but I have nothing here at all. I have nothing here but you, and now even you seem to be slipping away from me."

His anger diminishes, and he slowly sits at the table.

"We're not slipping," he argues. "But you're right. We are a bit stuck. I know that, and I apologize. Things will change."

He seems contrite, but something in his voice worries her. It's as if she is expected to agree with his assessment, and if she dares to disagree, his anger will return. She ends the conversation along with the dinner and makes herself busy in the room. If only they had a second room into which she could retreat.

For a fleeting moment, she has an image of her old farmhouse and the upstairs room where she would sometimes hide from Wayne.

Later that evening, she manages to stay awake, cleaning and reading until after Jeb has fallen asleep. He sits slightly upright in the bed, still wearing his clothes. When she finally rests, she does so in a stuffed chair near the window, curled up beneath her shawl.

Her mind is filled with images from her married life. Is this always the path? Is this where things have to lead when a woman deals with a man? The good days slowly merge into the dull days, and then the power struggles start. It's maddening to think that this is the only way that males and females can live together.

The bitter taste of her years with Wayne still linger. It's an acidic flavor that taints her affection. Maybe her judgment too. She saw Wayne's face for a moment when Jeb pounded the table. It's not a face she wants to see again. Not ever.

She feels like her mind is racing in the wrong direction, so she tries to rein it in. Jeb can be a good man. In many ways, he's not at all like Wayne, and she needs to remember that. He's given up many things in order to do the work that he's doing. Someone with his mind could have gone to school to become a lawyer if he chose to. He has the mind for it.

Perhaps, if they stay together, she will encourage him to take that path. Suddenly Amanda sits bolt upright in her chair, realizing something important. It could be the very reason that they're both stuck here right now.

This small city, this place in the mountains of Montana, represents the end of an era for Jeb. It may be his last big union negotiation as an independent organizer. If he really does have a job waiting for him in California, then it's a much different type of job and a different type of life. It would be one that he's not used to.

By agreeing to take a supervisor's position in a factory, he's ending a dream that he's followed for the past seven years. He's giving up the labor organizer life and becoming one of the very people he's been working to protect.

Maybe he's fearful about making the transition. Maybe he's not ready.

Maybe that's why they're lingering here.

She doesn't rise from her chair, but she looks toward the window and at the hilltops that remain visible in the moonlight. If he stays, this is the sort of town where there will always be a new dispute to settle. Always more workers to appease. It will never be a perfect time for Jeb to go. She may have to drag him away, and he'd better be ready to leave. That's the only way they'll ever continue their life together.

She settles back into the soft chair and closes her eyes.

A month and a half. That's all the time she's had to get to know this man. She's planning her life, and his life too, after knowing him for such a short period of time.

But so what? Doesn't she already feel better about Jeb than she ever felt bout Wayne?

That accounts for something, doesn't it?

This is a trying time for her, and none of the choices seem workable.

Chapter 24

A Change of Plans

"What the hell do you mean you're off the force?"

Devlin Richards gives Officer Hudson, now apparently *former* Officer Hudson, an incredulous look.

"I got caught boosting the stupid box you wanted me to grab. I can't believe I agreed to it." He shakes his head. "Such a stupid little thing. Who would have believed taking that stupid thing is what would end up getting me axed?"

The two men sit on a park bench, this time in broad daylight. Hudson wears plainclothes now, not a police uniform.

"I don't understand," Devlin replies. "How did they even catch you? You seem to be pretty careful with these things."

"Some damn new guy on the force. Likes to play strictly by the rules. I wasn't counting on that. I wasn't counting on anyone caring about it at all."

Devlin shakes his head. "This is not good news. Puts us back to square one."

"At least the good news to you is that someone finally managed to get the box out of that locked safe. I almost had it out of the station house too. We could have been free and clear if I'd made it.

"Did it look like it was still intact?"

"Sure was. I shook it a bit. Couldn't get it unlocked. There's some loose stuff inside it. Any idea what it might be?"

Devlin only shrugs.

"Tell you what I think they are … diamonds. Yes, sir. I've taken enough stolen merchandise from thieves. I know what diamonds sound like. Put a few loose diamonds in a cigar box, and they sound just like that."

Devlin smiles, but only on the inside.

"So what are you going to do now?" Hudson asks.

Devlin doesn't reveal what he'd really like to do. Many things cross his mind. He's not sure that he can trust this ex-cop, so one of his first thoughts is to kill him, then go to his place and search everywhere, to see if maybe he just kept the puzzle box. Maybe he is just lying about it.

Hum… but then why would he even mention diamonds?

As they talk, a woman approaches the bench. She's dressed in black with a large hat pulled low over her face. A dark lacy veil hangs from the front of the hat, obscuring her features. She looks like a woman in mourning, and she stands nearby, until Hudson starts eyeing her nervously.

"She's here to meet me," says Devlin. "Pay her no mind."

He can see that Hudson is skittish, and doesn't want to continue their conversation in front of another person. Devlin realizes it might be best, for now, to just keep

Hudson in his confidence. He could still use a partner in this effort, and an ex-cop surely would have some good contacts.

Devlin decides Hudson isn't savvy enough to do a double-cross on him, so he decides to continue their collaboration. Perhaps it's Jeb Thomas who needs to be cut out of the arrangement. Despite his occasional telegrams, the man has been absent for weeks.

"So where is the box now?" he asks in his southern drawl.

Hudson leans in and replies in very low whisper. "Still in the station house."

"What will they do with it?"

"Usual procedure is to give it back to its owner."

Devlin Richards nods. "Okay then. Here's what we're going to do …."

They make plans for about 20 minutes, then Devlin heads out of the park, walking slowly with the woman in black. They head back to his place, and once they're alone, the black veil is removed. Irene smiles at him, and they kiss passionately. She can't afford to be seen with him. But she doesn't want to stay away entirely.

Devlin doesn't want that either. And the next half hour shows him exactly why.

Chapter 25

Union Action

Slick mud coats the bottoms and sides of Amanda's shoes. Widening her stance, she steadies herself and makes her way across the street toward the protection of a wooden overhang in front of a general store in downtown Butte. Six other people already lurk beneath the eaves. They look toward where the setting sun should be, but only the vaguest hint of light is visible through the storm clouds.

"Good six hours of rain and it's still falling," mumbles an old man. "Ain't going to let up anytime soon." He's sort of directing his comment to her, but talks loudly enough for the whole group to hear. An anemic attempt at conversation for a group of people whose only common bond is that they're trapped by the driving rain.

Someone else speaks up. "Going to flood the damn mines if this keeps up." The voice comes from a man who appears to be the storekeeper, his white apron stained with grease and blood and a pencil tucked behind one ear.

"That ain't going to be any good for any of us," someone else grumbles.

Amanda looks through her purse for a head scarf. Lightning strikes a few miles in the distance, and someone on the porch *yee-haws* at its flash.

She turns to the shopkeeper and asks, "Do you know how I get to the Orphean Hall?"

"Huh? What do you want to go there for?"

"There's a Butte Workingman's Union meeting being held there this evening."

The old man overhears the question and sneers. "Union? You a union girl there, missy?" He cackles like a deranged rooster.

She ignores him and tells the shopkeeper that she needs to meet a friend at the hall. He points and describes a building that's about three blocks away. Quick motions with his hands tell her where to turn and what to avoid, given the state of the roads.

"You got an umbrella?"

"I'm afraid I don't, no, sir."

A distant bolt of lightning illuminates the sky.

He looks at her meager scarf and shakes his head. As Amanda turns to leave, he asks her to wait a moment. Something paternal and caring registers in his voice. Stepping into his shop, he returns with a two-by-two-foot piece of waxed paper. "Best I can offer you for free," he says. "But it may keep ya covered."

She thanks him and holds the paper over her head. As she hurries down the street, the rain falls even harder, and she literally runs toward the meeting, skidding, slipping, and hopping over piles of horse and donkey dung.

Jeb doesn't know she's coming to the meeting. She's only seen him speak a couple times, and she wants to do so again. He says he doesn't like to have her watch. Makes him feel nervous and silly.

But watching him speak tonight just seems like the right thing to do. Perhaps it will give her a sense of whether he's wrapping up his work in the town, or if he's still deep in the throes of it. She has to know.

This morning she found an old telegram, sent to someone in Boston. She's not totally sure, but it seemed to be referencing her, and her lost puzzle box. But it didn't seem like Jeb was trying to help recover the item. It seemed like he was more interested in the box's contents.

The wording was vague, but the more she thought about it, the more troubling it seemed.

Arriving at the hall, she sees the place is packed, and the excess audience has spilled out into the street. Men lurk in groups of threes and fours. There are a few women too, since some of the older men have brought their wives.

"What they saying in there?" someone asks. "Can't hear a damn thing with this rain."

"Sayin' they's gunna make a stand," someone else replies. "Make it right away. I heard that much over all the clapping."

"Yeah? 'Bout time then, I say. More than about time. They do that, I'm with 'em."

Amanda walks slowly through the crowd, catching snippets of conversations here and there.

"It's a fine mess, eh? And it sure ain't going to end anytime soon."

"Don't know why the local government puts up with 'em. That's where we need to start, not with the Chinamen themselves, eh? Get the town leaders on our side, they'll do something."

"You damn fool. That ain't going to work. The mine bosses outright own the government here. They ain't going to do a damn thing to help the likes of us. It's all about money. Always is."

"It's up to us, the miners, to do something."

"Yeah, but how?"

"Well …." Amanda sees the man spit tobacco juice onto the wet sidewalk. "I reckon that's what we're here to see. We need some ideas and we need 'em right fast."

Amanda tries, with little luck, to slip into the hall through the main door. There just isn't room. But she can hear a scraping noise around the corner, and she realizes someone is propping open a side door to increase ventilation in the big meeting room. Amanda holds the wet wax paper over her head and slips around the corner.

"I know what I'd do. Bust some heads," she hears someone say in passing. "You know that's what them damn Chinamen need, right? A busted head or two? Make examples out of a few of them and the whole lot will hightail it outta here faster'n grease lightning."

She hears grunts of agreement from the other men.

Inside the side door, Amanda finds a small space and stands on her tiptoes to see over the other meeting attendees. There must be 300 people inside. Jeb is wrapping up his speech. She sees high-ranking local union officials standing on each side of him. They look angry, and so does

167

Jeb. But they also look weary, like they're carrying the weight of a terrible task with them, and they're not happy to shoulder the burden.

"Who's with us then!?" one of the union officials shouts. A roar rises from the crowd.

"Who's it going to be?" shouts the other. "Us or them? Who's going to own this work? Who's entitled to it?"

The shouting and clapping slowly evolve into a rhythmic stomping of feet. Soon the whole crowd is chanting some phrase that Amanda can't make out. It's a rhyme of sorts, recited with fists in the air. The three men on the stage, with Jeb in the center, clasp hands and hold them over their heads.

Soon the crowd spills back into the street, still clapping and still chanting. It's like the rain isn't even happening. The crowd seems oblivious to the storm. They're taking part in some kind of war dance that winds through the streets of Butte.

Amanda grows fearful but stays with the group. Part of her wants to see where this is heading, and part of her simply wants to be nearby in case something happens to Jeb. In this frenzy, it seems like anything at all could happen.

She manages to spot Jeb walking near the front of the pack. He seems to be stoking the very frenzy that she fears.

Several of the men hold long sticks and boards now. Others pick up items as they march. Metal poles. Old tools. Someone hands out lengths of rope with pieces of iron tied to the ends. Buckets full of burning rags are held on the ends of sticks. The group marches until they come to a storefront with hand-painted Chinese writing on the window. Someone tosses a brick through the glass. Then one of the flaming buckets of rags is thrown through the opening. In less than a minute, the whole front end of the shop is ablaze.

The group moves on. A Chinese worker unlucky enough to wander out from a side street crosses their path. His eyes widen at what he sees. He is grabbed by his arms and someone starts to ask him a question. He's expected to answer to this self-appointed court. But before the answer comes, a fat board strikes the man on the side of his head. He slumps to the ground, the dark braid on the back of his head trailing red into the gutter. There's laughter as someone kicks him twice in the stomach.

"You see that? You see that, Mr. Thomas?" The question comes from one of the men who stood with Jeb in the meeting hall. "That's what we're talking about. That's what we gotta do. Hit a few of them upside the head and these people are gunna take us seriously now, eh?"

Amanda holds her hand over her mouth, ready to scream at what she's seen. Jeb turns around and nods to the men. The injured Chinaman is dragged aside, and the mob continues down the street. She wants to help the poor soul. But, even more, she wants to either protect Jeb, or find out if he's acting as a catalyst for this violence. Christian duty getting the better of her, she kneels beside the injured man, holding his head in her hands.

Amanda's mind reels. She can't believe what she's seen. Is Jeb leading this terrible mob? Does he really comprehend the nasty nature of what these men are doing?

Someone comes out of the side street and runs to help the man in the gutter. It's a Chinese woman who casts an angry eye at Amanda. Others follow, and they all stare at her.

Instinct overcomes her desire to help and she runs, finding herself again at the rear of the angry mob. She follows silently and watches the front line of the group.

It does indeed appear that Jeb approves of the mob's violent actions. Two more men are beaten senseless. In the occasional burst of lightning, she can make out Jeb's silhouette. He's pointing. In another flash, she sees him land a few punches himself, one with a blow that sends a man toppling backwards, his black middle-parted butt-cut hair whipping in the breeze.

Amanda has seen enough. She lingers near the rear of the crowd, then rushes back to help the poor injured man as the group moves on. He's dazed as she sits him up, holding a handkerchief to his bleeding nose. She feels safer here because there's no one else coming to his aid.

"Why are they doing this to you?" she asks as she helps him to his feet. Though she pretty much knows the answer.

The man's English is not good, but he tells her what he can. The problem is the jobs, he says. With a steady stream of workers to choose from, the mine owners keep cutting wages, and hundreds of Chinese men, having completed work on a nearby rail line, keep wandering into Butte and showing up at the mines.

They're so desperate for work that the lower wages seem fine to them. They're happy to take the jobs. The older workers, some with families to support, are upset about that.

The tension in town has been unbearable lately. Amanda has felt it herself. The only thing that has kept it from boiling over is the drinking, gambling, and whoring that takes place at night. But the tension remains, and no one should be surprised that things are coming to a head.

"We need eat too!" the Chinaman says, dabbing at his face. "We take jobs. Pay is pay. What else we do?"

As she walks him toward his home, she hears more windows shattering in the distance, then police whistles. The crowd appears to be scattering. The union isn't going to battle the police directly. At least not yet. Nor will they burn any more shops tonight.

The message has been sent, and it's an important one. The union has put the Chinese and the mine owners on notice that they intend to fight the current situation, by any means necessary.

Chapter 26

Electric Kid

Victor and Thurman arrive at the location of the Friday night fights. It's about an hour before the start time. Two pubs located in the same block already have good crowds. Victor can hear boasts and betting. The air is humid and dank with the smell of horse dung and stale beer.

They set up a small table just to the right of the front door to the warehouse. They need to be far enough away that the fight managers don't run them off, but close enough to be noticed by the crowd.

Victor was able to acquire seven large batteries from MIT. He slides them beneath the table. Thurman covers the top with a blue cloth.

Victor crawls under the table and takes four of the batteries, setting them aside in two pairs. First, each pair is wired in a parallel circuit, which doubles the capacity of a single battery. Then the two groups of two are wired in a larger series-style circuit. That essentially doubles the voltage. The effect will be a more powerful jolt than what he has been able to deliver before from a single battery. And the extra capacity, hopefully, will make the charge last longer.

"Think we'll be able to get several fights out of this?" Thurman asks.

"Don't know. Hope so. I don't even know if we'll get any takers at all, so it could be a moot point."

Thurman just winks and replies, "You just leave that to me."

Victor takes the remaining three batteries and wires them in a separate series circuit. This is his back-up plan. He attaches a separate set of wires to this group.

The first part of their work completed, they walk to one of the nearby pubs, where Victor downs two shots of whiskey. Then they grab some beers and head back to the table. Jimmy and Lucas have arrived. They all step behind a pile of crates located near the table, and they set out some basic plans.

Victor is wearing a boxer's outfit beneath his clothes. It's really just some stretchy pants and a pair of ankle-high athletic shoes that he found at a secondhand store. He'll go shirtless and do some shadow boxing while Thurman calls out for challengers. As Thurman lays out his part of the plan, Victor strips down then pulls not one but two pairs of heavy rubber gloves over his hands. With both pairs in place, his hands look a bit like they're covered by puffy boxing gloves. Close enough, anyway.

Thurman talks directly to Jimmy and Lucas. "So, while I'm calling out for challengers for Victor, you two just walk by and stop to listen. Just mill about. Hopefully we'll get more of a crowd that way."

The two men nod.

"Might be that's all we need you to do. But if there are no takers, then we'll need you gentlemen to step in. Start talking up the idea. Say stuff like 'That sort of power won't be enough to hurt anyone.' Or 'a good fighter should be able to take a couple of hits.' That sort of thing."

"Okay," says Lucas. He doesn't seem convinced.

While they talk, Victor starts attaching the wires to himself. He starts with the wires that come from the four batteries. The cables stretch out from under the table and snake up Victor's right leg. He attaches them with a few rubber bands. The insulated wires wrap around his waist and run up his back. Thurman secures them in place with thick brown packing tape. At Victor's shoulders, the wires split – one wire down each arm. These too are held in place with loose bands attached to his elbows and wrists. The last part of the wire, below the wrists, is stripped bare right about where the gloves start. The bare wires are then attached to the knuckles of the rubber gloves. He has a set of wires on each hand, so that an electric punch can be delivered from the left or the right.

Now it's time for the second set of wires.

Victor has devised a creative plan. The wires that attach to the second group of batteries are set up in a way that makes them a bit more powerful. One wire runs to each hand and they are attached to the ends of his thumbs.

While the first set of wires create a circuit when he punches with a single fist, the second set of wires won't create a complete circuit unless he touches his opponent with both hands. It's designed to be a last-ditch, close-in tool. It's something he can pull out of his bag of tricks – but only if needed.

With everything in place, Victor does a little shadow boxing, quickly swinging some one-two combinations. Satisfied that the wires are tight, he reaches under the table and screws down a nut. He is live, electrified, and ready.

Jimmy shakes his head. "Okay... I think this is probably the most far-fetched thing I've ever been involved with," he laughs. "Are you guys good runners? Because if we piss anyone off, we'll all need to hightail it out of here pretty damn fast."

Thurman waves off the concern. "We'll be fine. We're making no claim other than you can get a jolt to your jaw. You can show your friends how tough you are." He tells Jimmy and Lucas to head up the street to wait. They should slowly walk toward the table once they hear him making his announcements. Then Thurman looks at Victor, who nods. Everyone takes a deep breath, and they start.

Thurman steps forward, holds up his arms and slowly spins around. "Ladies and gentlemen!" he starts. It doesn't matter that the crowd is mostly men, and it doesn't matter that virtually no one pays him any mind. Thurman keeps his voice loud and steady. He's hoping that his sense of authority, such as it is, will draw people in. Victor also raises his gloves over his head, then quickly touches the tips of the two wires together. Sparks fly. People jump. A few people stop to look and Victor nods at them, with a sly wink.

The street where the warehouse sits is more industrial than commercial. No stores. Just hulking brick buildings and the shoddy drinking establishments. The fronts of these buildings have metal doors and few windows. But the desolation has a new façade. Because the Friday night fights have been held here for several months, the street has received a new skin. Advertising posters have appeared on buildings and fences – stacked three high in some places.

Highland Springs Brewery. Witch Cream aftershave lotion. *Bayer Cough Suppressant with Heroin.* There are even posters with delivery price lists from lumber yards and coal suppliers. Most are big black and white prints, but they have colored paint slapped around the edges or flags tacked to the tops to help draw attention.

On fight nights like this, the grimy street takes on a carnival atmosphere. Newsboys shout. Fiddle players call out jigs, their cases open for coins. Black-clad men, flat caps pulled low, sell twisted stems of bhang in darkened doorways.

"Ladies and gentlemen," Thurman calls again, "step up and see the strangest manner of fight you have ever witnessed, in this age or any age. This man here is tackling a new and dangerous way of fighting tonight. I'll tell you this, my good people. We are strictly off card tonight – because there is no way this experimental and electrifying event would ever be allowed inside the building!"

People do stop. The words are compelling. The shirtless and newly beefy Victor Marius, punching at the air and trailing wires, catches people's eyes. The small crowd quickly grows from four people to nine, then close to 20. Victor touches the wires together again, and the flying sparks elicits oohs and aahs from the group. Some people step back in fear.

Up the block, Jimmy and Lucas can see that they will not need to help create the crows. So they walk to the back of the group and start making loud comments about the display.

"That's amazing."

"How does he do that?"

"What in the world are those wires?"

"Is that safe? How can that be safe?"

Their comments are cartoonish and basic, yet people seem to be caught up in the moment. They too are looking on in awe and making comments of their own.

Thurman calls for someone to challenge Victor. "Can you take an electric punch? Are you tough enough to take not just a sock on the jaw, but a shock too? Can you beat the Electric Kid?"

Victor gives Thurman a quizzical look about name, but Thurman shrugs.

"That's... that's right! The Electric Kid! It's shocking how well he fights. He's electrifyingly punched people from New Orleans to Montreal. He's left his mark on big jaws to small. Won't anyone challenge the man? Bet one dollar! If you win, you get three back! That's how confident we are that you can't beat the kid!"

Behind the growing crowd, Jimmy whispers to Lucas. What if he loses? How much money do we have to pay folks off?"

"Between us? I think we have $14 dollars."

Jimmy shakes his head. "This is crazy." He thinks for a minute, then whispers into Lucas' ear. "You know what? Start taking bets. I'm going to take the bait, and then I'll take a fall."

Jimmy loops around to the far side of the crowd, then steps up in front of Victor. "I'll take him on! I'm not afraid of those silly sparks." He slaps a dollar down on the table and starts to raise his fists. Lucas calls out from the back of the crowd.

"I've got even money that says the challenger loses."

The crowd laughs. "You'd better offer better odds than that, sonny!" shouts a man in a bowler.

"Three to one?"

"Make it five to one, and I'll put down $20."

"Done," says Lucas. He pushes to the front of the crowd and stands near the table. Money changes hands, and he finds an old crate to hold the bets.

With one bet down, others follow. Soon they have close to seventy dollars wagered. Jimmy makes sure he puts on a good show. He sets to it with a solid boxing stance, swears a few times, and states that he's not afraid of the electric wires. The two spin, jab and parry, always careful to step over the wires. Jimmy jabs hard once, catching Victor under the chin. But Victor steps back, absorbing the blow. The crowd cheers. They do a few more jabs, then Victor throws a fast right uppercut. He pulls most of the force at the last second, but it still catches Jimmy sharply on the left side of his jaw. The scientist makes sure that two wires connect with the skin, completing the circuit. There's a slight buzz, and Jimmy yelps. He staggers back.

"Fuck! That really stung!" He shakes his head and rubs his face. He looks at Victor, who quickly realizes that he hurt his friend a lot more than either anticipated. Still, Jimmy raises his hands again and steps gamely forward. Victor punches a few more times, twisting his hand slightly each time, so that the wires don't connect when he slightly hits Jimmy's jaw. Jimmy makes a slight buzzing sound with his mouth to fake the sound of the quick electric connection. People aren't familiar enough with the sound of electricity to tell what's real and what's not. After about five punches, Victor realizes they're pushing their luck. He connects again with the wires, and Jimmy yelps. There's a two-inch red mark on his cheek, and the smell of burning flesh fills the air. He looks shocked and angry.

He rushes in for a clench and speaks into Victor's ear as Victor fake-wrestles to break the hold. "We need to end this. I'm not taking another one of your damn punches." Through gritted teeth, he mutters "one, two three." Victor places a hand against his neck. Both the men hiss and buzz slightly through their teeth. The effect is believable enough. Jimmy jumps a bit, falls backwards and grabs his neck. A roar goes up from the crowd. Jimmy waves off his opponent. He's done.

More people gather as Thurman raises Victor's hand. Lucas gathers the winnings, and more people step forward. Two men say they want to try their hand at fighting, and they put up their money. More people step up to wager. Lucas reduces the odds to three to one, claiming that Victor has already proven he can win, so he's now more of a favorite.

The next match will be Victor's first legitimate fight as the Electric Kid, even though he has not yet fully embraced the name. The man who steps up is tall and powerful-looking. But he's also obviously drunk. He's been goaded into the fight by some friends. Victor decides to stay in place for this bout. He doesn't want the fool tripping over his wires if they circle each other. Plus, making the other fighter do the moving will let him judge how coordinated he is.

"Give him hell, Tommy!" One of the man's friends shouts. "Shove those wires down his throat!"

Tommy leads with his left. Bare fists jabbing several times while keeping his right cocked and ready for a big hit. The man obviously has some fight experience, yet he is slow and ponderous in his movements. Victor blocks several of the jabs. One gets through and connects with his nose. As he shakes it off, Tommy's big meaty right hook sails in from the side. But Victor turns his fingers toward it, so that the fist lands right on the exposed wires. There's a sizzle. Tommy

180

staggers to the side. His burned knuckles fly to his mouth as he looks at Victor, confused. Victor realizes this man probably doesn't know much at all about electricity.

"Had enough?"

"I ain't backing down from the likes of you!" Tommy sneers. He moves in, and after swinging wildly several times, he manages to connect, hard, with Victor's rib cage. Victor winces. He quickly hits back, slamming the big man hard in the cheek and knocking him back two steps. The wires rip loose from Victor's glove, and dangle harmlessly out of the way.

"Hang on!" Thurman calls out "Need to make a repair."

"The hell you do!" The other fighter shouts back. We keep going." The crowd cheers, obviously on the side of the challenger. Thurman looks to Lucas, but he shrugs. The man who takes the bets has to appear neutral.

Tommy lunges forward again. Victor thinks about relying on his back-up plan, the other three batteries, but he holds back. Tommy may be big, but all of his swings have come toward Victor in the exact same way. Victor stands sideways and is able to transfer his weight quickly and pull his head back two, then three times as Tommy's impressive but wild swings fail to connect. Tommy shifts his weight to try a new approach, and Victor takes that opportunity to throw his weight behind an uppercut. It hits Tommy hard and makes him stagger backwards. When he reaches a curb, he falls, striking his head. He's out cold.

The cheers grow louder. More bets take place as Thurman tapes Victor's wires back into place. Behind them, someone in the door of the warehouse takes notice, looks out at the crowd in the street, then disappears inside.

Victor is tired and his chest hurts. But his heart is thumping hard as the haze of the drugs and the thrill of winning give him a burst of energy. He calls for more challengers.

The next man to step up is obviously in much better shape than Tommy. He moves fast. But he lacks the boxing experience that Victor saw in the bigger man. He doesn't lead with jabs. He leaves himself unprotected. To save the juice of the battery, Victor decides to fight this guy without using the electricity. He blocks blow after blow, then shoots out jabs when the man drops his guard. He connects with a crack. It looks brutal, but this fight is actually somewhat easy. All show and no real impact. When the man's left arm drops a bit for the third time, Victor drives his fist hard into the man's left eye socket. He staggers back and waves his hands. He's done.

More cheers.

"Don't be fighting like that!" someone yells. "We want to see some sparks!" Victor laughs and slams the tops of his fists together. Sparks do fly again and the crowd cheers. There's over 100 people gathered now. They don't go inside to watch the other fights. And that's a problem. A group of men have come out of the building to watch, and they are not happy with the business competition.

Victor takes on two more comers, one after the other. Both are put up to it by friends. They aren't really into fighting and the bouts don't last long. A couple of good shocks sends both howling back to their laughing groups.

Even these short, almost comical bouts have given Victor a renewed respect for real boxers. Just the act of holding one's hands up protectively, and punching occasionally, can be very taxing on the body. Combine that with being hit on occasion, and it is exhausting work.

As he catches his breath, a tall man with a long reach slaps his money down on the table, then rolls up his sleeves.

Victor knows immediately that this will be the toughest opponent he will have faced. The man looks like he spends his day lifting hay bales and his nights brawling in bars. He has scars, a flat nose, and a sneer that says *I've done this before and I'm good at it.*

Action at the betting table suddenly increases. Victor touches his fingers together and notices that the sparks have dimmed a bit. He looks at Thurman. Not much either of them can do.

Stepping toward the big man, Victor takes up his fighting stance. He avoids two jabs then takes the third right on his collarbone. It's a big jolt and it seriously hurts.

As the man moves in to connect again, Victor hits him with a quick one-two punch. He can see that the man feels the shocks, and that they are a surprise to him. But they are not powerful enough to make him back off.

Victor suddenly catches a hard right to his stomach and he feels it all the way to his back. It's the sort of blow that can turn intestines to liquid. He winces, and realizes that he needs to do something to take this guy out fast. He's not going to win against him if they are just going blow by blow.

One more hard swing by the big man. Victor dodges it and gets him in a clinch. Quickly, he twists his hand so that the single wire on his right hand, the one connected to the triple back-up battery bank, is resting right against the man's neck. Then he pushes his left fist right into the crook of the man's elbow. This closes the circuit. The current passes through the man's neck, chest and arm.

The man grunts and tries to break the hold. But the wires burn and shock. Since Victor is in contact with the man's skin, he can feel some of the shock too. It's not enough to kill, but it's a hell of a jolt to someone who was not expecting it. Victor feels him cough and shutter. They push apart and Victor gives a final hard punch as a going-away present. The man falls back onto his ass. He shakes his head and rubs the burned spot on the back of his neck.

"You fucking bastard!" he stammers. "You're cheating!"

"Cheating?" Victor shouts back "I'm doing the exact thing I said I would do. I'm wired up! Apparently, I'm the goddamn Electric Kid. You knew that!"

The man grunts and rises to his feet. He's unsteady. He looks angry, but also very cautious. He half-heartedly starts throwing jabs again but keeps his distance from Victor, weary of another clinch.

Victor swings and finally connects again, hitting the man in the nose. In return, he receives a bruising punch on the side of his shoulder. But the man finally throws his hands up and backs off, none too soon. Blood gushes from his nose.

Thurman starts his spiel again, looking for more challengers. But they hear whistles and shouts. Cops are pushing their way through the crowd with billy clubs drawn.

Victor's opponent has been putting his shirt back on, but he suddenly disappears. It's as if he was swallowed up by the crowd. Victor catches just one more glimpse of him, at a distance now, walking fast with hands thrust into his pockets and head turned away from the police he is obviously hoping to avoid.

"Who's running this little show?" A sergeant demands.

Victor says nothing. He just smiles. With his hands fully wired, he's obviously involved.

"I guess we are," says Thurman.

"All right then, why don't you just tell me what's going on?"

Thurman takes the straightforward approach. This is just an exhibition, he explains. People are curious about electricity. Their little demonstration shows the crowd that it's both a little dangerous, and maybe not so dangerous. After all, everyone has survived the punch.

As he Thurman and the officers talk, Victor starts removing his gloves and the wires. Someone tries to grab some money back from the betting table, and Victor shouts and flattens him. The police intervene and push the crowd back a few feet.

To Victor's surprise, some people from the gathered crowd actually speak up in their defense.

"We was enjoying the show!" says a man in blue overalls.

"Yeah, no harm done. Let 'em be," says a man in a tweed cap.

By the time the police turn to him, Victor has started packing up his equipment.

"And what's your story?" the sergeant demands.

Victor shrugs. "I don't have a story. I just build stuff, and sometimes it works."

The policemen squint at him. They look angry. But just then, the call goes out from the warehouse doorway. The fights are starting. The crowd starts to move inside, though a few men stay behind, curious as to where this little altercation will lead.

"Ahh, you're working for them," one of the men in the crowd mutters to the cops as he gestures toward the building. "Guess they ain't liking the competition, so you come along and shut these boys down."

"You mind your mouth!" the other cop replies, reaching for his club. But the sergeant holds up his hand and tries to cool things a bit.

"You can't run your little sideshow here anymore, boys. Got it? You need a license."

"A license?" Thurman retorts. "No one here has a license! Everything on this street is off the books, including the fights inside."

"You're on the street, not in the building. And the streets are my business. Now get your asses out of here, and I don't want to see you back next week."

Victor starts to move his batteries, but the cop says no. "Those stay, until I can investigate them and decide whether they are legal to own."

Victor starts to argue, but Thurman pulls him away. They'll never see that rig again. It's the cost of doing business.

The good news is, when they count their winnings later that night, there's a few hundred dollars to split. Victor gets 50%, for coming up with the equipment and taking the punches. Thurman gets 30% for being the carnival barker, and Jimmy and Lucas get 10% each, for milling about and helping stoke the crowd. With no batteries to use again, and since their fighting scheme won't be as big a surprise to the crowd a second time around, they realize that they will have to retire the Electric Kid after just one outing.

"It was a good run while it lasted!" Victor says, hoisting a glass.

"Shocked that we even got away with it," says Thurman.

Chapter 27

Breaking Away

Arriving back at the rooming house, the first thing Amanda does is look up at her own window. It remains dark, which probably means Jeb is still out. That's good because it will give her time to pack her things.

Still, she treads cautiously up the stairs, just in case he's hiding there in the dark, watching for the police or some real or imagined enemy.

The room is indeed empty. She lights a lamp, keeps the flame low, and begins to pack, throwing clothes and shoes haphazardly into her leather satchel. Her first thought is just to disappear into the night, but that would be cowardly. She should at least leave Jeb a note.

It would be even less cowardly to confront him and tell him why she's leaving, but she's too worried for her own safety to do that. She's seen his anger recently, and she knows that he's capable of violence. And the memory of her problems with Wayne remain all too fresh.

She finds some scrap paper in a wastebasket and starts to write.

Dear Jeb.

I apologize for leaving this note for you instead of saying good-bye in person, but I think it's best this way. While these past several weeks with you have been wonderful, they have also been quite troubling for me. It's become obvious to me that your work is one of the most important things in your life. Because of that, building something beyond that work life seems difficult for you. We have lingered here in Butte for far too long. I see no real desire on your part to move on with me to San Francisco. Despite what you say, I don't think you are ready to give up the life of a labor organizer.

But that's not the main reason I'm leaving. I saw what you and the other union organizers did tonight, Jeb, and I was shocked by it. I can't live with a man who has such a violent capacity in his heart. I do understand the struggle you are facing, but I could never defend the way you have chosen to achieve your goals.

You beat a man severely tonight. After you and the crowd moved on, I helped him. That is the difference between the two of us right now, Jeb. You and I have a far different idea of what it means to help people, and far different ideas about who actually deserves help. I think it's too wide a gap for us to ever close.

Regretfully,

Amanda

She tucks the letter under the corner of the lamp, then grabs her satchel. Just as she reaches the top of the stairs, she hears the doorlatch click. There are voices below, and one of them is Jeb's.

"I think we're okay here for a while," he whispers. "We'll just hide out upstairs. Not many people know where I live. I've always kept it quiet."

Amanda ducks back down the hall and steps into the last empty room on the left.

The men plod up the stairs and into one of the other vacant rooms. The room remains dark, and she can hear them standing near the window, looking out.

"Ain't no one following us," one of the men whispers. "Chinamen ain't got the guts right now, and the police don't care, long as we've stopped."

"Maybe," Jeb replies, "but we still need to be careful."

There's a long period of silence. Amanda finds herself leaning forward, listening intently. Finally, she hears someone say, "Got any whiskey?"

The men sit near the window and drink. Jeb wanders into their bedroom, and she can hear him read the note. In a few minutes, he rushes back to the room and says that he has to go out.

"Out? Are you a damn fool? We came up here to lie low for a bit!"

"It's Amanda. It's my …." He struggles for a word and finally picks one that makes Amanda shake her head in dismay. "My fiancé," he says. "I just need to check … I'll be back."

He runs down and out of the building. Amanda sits on the edge of the other room's unmade bed, suitcase on her lap and hands folded on top. She knows where he's going. He's headed to the train station to try to stop her. It's the only easy way to leave town if you don't own a horse. Amanda waits several minutes, then walks slowly toward the window, taking her time with each step to minimize the squeaking of the floorboards. She waits until she sees Jeb coming back toward the building, then she makes her move, tiptoeing into the hall.

She and Jeb have always used the back staircase. But at the front of the third floor, there is a door that leads to a small landing near the top of the main hotel staircase. The door was locked when they arrived, but Jeb told her it would be safer if they had a second exit. He borrowed a key and unlocked it, though they never used those stairs.

As Jeb reaches the back stairs, Amanda pulls open the door and steps onto the front landing. She uses the noise Jeb makes as he runs up the stairs to cover the sound of her own descent. At the second floor, there is a carpet runner on the treads, and the rest of her departure is nice and quiet.

According to the tall clock in the front hallway of the building, it's nearly 11:00 p.m.

Out on the streets, things are quiet. The few people out walking peer at each other suspiciously and avoid getting too close. Lingering distrust from the evening's events.

At least, the rain has let up.

For the past months, she has heard a train whistle each night right at eleven. That's when the day's last train departs the station, headed for Denver.

She has a few dollars tucked into the front pocket of her suitcase. If she hurries, she should be able to make that train.

Running through the mud with a heavy bag is surprisingly tiring. Amanda finds herself panting as she reaches the station. She can hear the locomotive idling and hissing just outside the wide backdoors. Out of the corner of her eye, she can also see a freight train gliding slowly along a siding near the edge of the railyard. It stops near the station's water tower.

"One ticket to Denver, please," she says upon reaching the ticket window.

The ticket agent just stares at her. "Are you Ms. Grant?"

She says nothing.

"You are, aren't you?"

As she looks into the station agent's eyes, she realizes she's made a terrible mistake. When Jeb came here looking for her, he also must have asked them to keep an eye out for her. He has friends throughout the railroad.

"Umm …." She wants to lie and say no, but it's not going to do her much good.

"I'm sorry, miss, but I can't let you on the train."

She looks at him coldly. "I beg your pardon?"

"You heard me. Jeb has asked that you remain in town. Once the train leaves, I'm happy to escort you back to your place of lodging, if you'd like."

"No, I wouldn't like that at all," she replies. "How about if I have you escort me to the police station so that I can file a complaint for kidnapping?"

The agent looks surprised, but presses on with his collusion. "You have to understand, miss, the police will likely want you to remain here too. I understand you were a witness to a fight this evening, no?"

She glares at him. "If I'm a witness for anything, it's for the poor men who were beaten by a mob. Are you proud of your friend Jeb? Do you want me to stay here and be a witness against him? And maybe you too?"

The man shrugs. "I don't care what you do tomorrow. But for tonight, I'm not going to let you on that train."

He walks out of his ticket booth and reaches for her bag. "I'll just keep this locked up until Jeb comes for you."

Amanda grabs the bag too, and a fight ensues. She kicks at his shins and holds her own in the struggle until the commotion draws a conductor who had been waiting out near the train.

He rushes to his colleague's aid, and Amanda lets go, backing toward the door.

"You see that woman?" the ticket agent shouts to the conductor. "She is NOT to get on the train. Do you understand?" He says something that she doesn't understand, but which she takes to be a union code word.

The conductor nods.

"Not on that train under any circumstances. She's wanted for questioning."

"Well then, why don't you just keep her here?" the conductor smiles. "I'll help you lock her up before the train leaves, if you want."

At that, Amanda bolts toward the door, leaving her suitcase and running around the outside of the building. Moving fast, she slips into a nearby woods before the two men appear at the door, laughing. She stumbles up a small hill and hides in a nest of saplings.

"Hell, I ain't going to chase her. It's wet out there and she's got nowhere to go. Let Jeb worry about her now."

The ticket agent heads back inside, and the conductor re-boards the train.

Amanda squats in the woods for a long time, trying to figure out what to do. All her money and worldly possessions, meager as they are, are in that bag. All she has left are the clothes on her back and her muddy shoes.

She watches as the train to Denver leaves the station right on time, and the building's lights go out shortly thereafter. From her hidden perch, she can see the ticket agent lock the door. He looks left, right, then up at the woods, before turning and heading down the street. It's then that she notices that he carries her suitcase with him. Her money along with it.

Much as she wants to go after it, she also knows this may be her only chance to leave. And leave she must. If Jeb is so controlling that he would prohibit her from boarding the train, then this isn't a place for her to stay.

She notices that the freight train still sits on the siding. It finishes taking on water. Working by the light of a red lantern, the engineer bolts down the water hatch and signals the fireman to stoke the fire. In about fifteen minutes, the engine starts to hiss. A new head of steam is building up.

Once the men climb back aboard the train, Amanda slips out of the woods and approaches the train cautiously. Most of the freight car doors are closed. Those that remain open are too close to the front of the train. She worries about being seen. But toward the back of the train is a cattle car. That will have to do. She runs to the open-sided structure just as the train releases its brakes and starts to roll away. Hoisting herself up and in, she can smell the acrid scent of cow dung. In the darkness, she hears nervous snorts and grunts from the animals. An intruder has joined them.

"Shhh," she whispers, using the same voice that she used to talk to her own cows. "I'm just going to ride with you for a while. Don't worry about me." She walks along, stroking long noses and patting rough hairy hide.

What is it, she wonders, that leads her to always find shelter and comfort amongst farm animals? For the third time in as many months, she's found solace in some kind of barnlike structure. She's always been running from a man and hiding among the stalls.

After her eyes adjust, she counts ten cows. They stand with their heads in small metal loops that keep them from falling over as the train lurches. She approaches the first cow and places her head on the animal's neck. She notices a full udder and realizes she will at least have something to drink.

"So tell me, Miss Cow, do you know where exactly this train is heading?"

Chapter 28

Evidence Returned

Jonathan Morgan carries Amanda's puzzle box back to his house as if he's carrying a trophy away from a sporting event. He smiles broadly, realizing that he's won.

He had to argue with the police officers at the station. The box was stolen from his house, he reminded them. It belonged to a friend of his, and he was the one most likely to find a way to return it to her.

Through the whole conversation, he was fearful that the police would put two and two together. They would realize that the owner of the box was Amanda, a woman for whom they had an arrest warrant on file. But the two incidents made no connection in the mind of the police captain at the station house. Eventually Jonathan just wore him down, and he let the old man take the box home.

What Morgan doesn't notice, as he walks along, is a man who lurks about a block behind him. The man who follows is gaunt in his face. Dark sunken eyes and severely underweight.

All it took was just a promise of a packet of opium and a meal to get him to watch the station house and to shadow Morgan when he left with the box.

When Jonathan Morgan returns to his fancy row house, the man waits for a moment to see if he re-emerges, then he writes down the number and slips away.

"Don't tell me," Beverly Morgan says with slight anger. "Please don't tell me that that's what I think it is."

Jonathan smiles. "They found it! The police, I mean. Turns out they had it all along. It was that shopkeeper character after all. He had it in his safe."

Beverly stares at the box like it's an evil demon.

"Why did you bring it back here?"

"Well, what else was I supposed to do with it? Give it away?"

She shakes her head in disgust. "I don't want that thing back here again, Jonathan. It's cursed. Someone broke into our home to take it once, and I'm worried about what might happen again."

"Don't you think we need to return it to its rightful owner?"

She eyes him coolly. "And how do you propose to do that?"

"Well, I'm not sure. I guess it just seems that she'll come looking for it at some point."

"I think you're a foolish old man. She's not coming back. She doesn't even know you have it. What are you going to do? Put it up in her room? Go to visit it now and then to make sure it's safe?"

"I think we should keep it right here in the parlor," he says. "I might like to try to figure the puzzle out myself."

Beverly lets him know in no uncertain terms that a "jewelry box" belonging to "that woman" will not be part of her formal parlor.

"What you're worried about is that you might see Amanda again. Isn't that what's going on?"

She gives her husband a cold look. "I'd like you to get rid of it. And you also need to get rid of that awful steam wagon that's still out in the carriage house. We need to be done with all of this."

Jonathan shakes his head as she walks away. But he realizes it might be time to pay a visit to his friend Jasper. Good old Jasper has such an interest in both the box and the steam car that he might be willing to store the items for a while. He might even be able to open some of the next levels on the box.

Across town, Devlin Richards holds up a small packet of opium and watches as the addict's eyes focus on it.

"What do you have to tell me?" he smiles.

"That box you want. It's not in the police station anymore. They let it go."

"They gave it to who? The owner? The girl?"

"No. I didn't see her at all. They gave it to the old man. The owner of that house. And it's back. Back at that house again."

Devlin smiles. Stealing it from that house the first time had been child's play.

"Any idea where they're keeping it?"

"No. Just saw him carry it through the front door."

Devlin nods and tosses the packet in the air. The addict snatches it and runs back to the dark basement where he lives. Back to his pipe and his strange blurred dreams.

Chapter 29

The Empty Plains

Amanda isn't certain, but instinct tells her that the train where she has stowed away is heading southeast. She makes no decision on whether the direction is a good thing or bad. She is heading away from Butte. She's directionless and penniless, so it's not clear which point of the compass rose holds the most promise.

Perhaps she has made a grave mistake. Perhaps she should have gone to the police. Would they have helped? Or would they, realizing she's associated with union agitators, have found a reason to throw her into jail? Yet is this a better alternative? To be riding into the night with no money and no plans?

She sits in a pile of straw, leaning against the outer boards of the cattle car. She tries to review how she ended up like this, hoping that will help her decide what to do next.

Her first thought was to leave Jeb and head to the nearest decent-sized city, maybe all the way back to Denver, where she would have many travel options. With the little bit of money she had, she could have found a place to stay and kept on there long enough to get her bearings. There would have been lots of options in a place like Denver. There were hotels where she could work. Maybe in a few weeks, she could have taken a train either east or west, depending on her mood.

She could still do that, couldn't she? No matter what town she ended up in on this train, she could surely find a church or a police officer. She could beg for a meal and enough charity to get her to a larger city.

All of these ideas help her form the basis of her plan. Outright begging, if she has to, and she will make her way to Denver. Or maybe Cheyenne. From there, she will use her wits to get back on her feet.

And from there? That is the interesting part to her. The longer term holds a strange sense of freedom that pushes aside her doubts.

There certainly is some attraction to continuing on, maybe building a new life in California. Or she could head back east. At least she knows a few people in Massachusetts, she knows what to expect there, and she certainly has a new confidence to help sustain her.

She sways side to side as the train rattles on.

In some ways, heading back east is the slightly more attractive option. And the steam car that was given to her is still there on the Morgans' property. In its beat-up condition, it isn't worth much, so she has never thought about selling it. Now, claiming it and selling it for even a few dollars sounds attractive.

She closes her eyes, realizing that she doesn't need to make her decision just yet. Soon her thoughts turn in a different direction. She finds her anger growing, and it's focused on that blasted ticket agent.

He took her bag! What gave him the right to do that? And with it went her money, her clothes, everything. What had he expected her to do? Stay there despite the violent nature of the man she lived with? Was she supposed to remain in town and be controlled by Jeb and his associates? Become a virtual prisoner?

No. I did the right thing by leaving. Maybe not by boarding this train so quickly. But I was right to leave him. She was too independent to stay as a prisoner. So she ran. She ran to here, wherever here was.

Feeling restless, she stands and paces the car. She finds a bucket of grain and feeds the cattle. Then she places her head against the side of one of the cows, half hugging it in frustration. Deep below the animal's leathery skin and hair, she can hear the beat of its heart and the growl of a stomach.

"I don't know what your name is, cow, or even if you have one. But I need a friend right now. I'm in trouble. I don't know where I am, I don't have any money, and I don't know where I'm going."

She pats the cow with affection. "But I guess I'm not that much different from you, am I? And you don't seem bothered by your predicament at all."

Settling back down, she tries to fall asleep, but bleak reality haunts her. Eventually she settles for a series of short dozes, interrupted each time the train jostles, bumps, or whistles. She feels the train slow down as it passes through towns. She feels the speed and the friction of the brakes as they head down the mountains and into the elevated plains. The train travels throughout the night, stopping once for water and coal. She thinks of jumping off there, but sees no buildings or lights at all. She finally falls asleep near dawn.

The sun is bright outside when Amanda is awakened by the sound of an opening door. Someone is coming in.

She curses herself for being fully asleep and not paying attention to the rhythms of the train. She has no idea what time it is or how far they have traveled. They're probably in Wyoming, but where?

Her plan had been to wait until the train stopped, and then look for a way off. If she was fast enough, she figured no one would spot her.

But she was asleep when they stopped. Now, her only option is to slide back into the shadows of the livestock car and wait. She's heard stories about the nature of railroad workers and how they treat stowaways. They bust heads. They have people arrested.

She's not keen on being discovered.

"Come on, cow. Move your fat ass!" someone shouts. Amanda peeks out.

If the cows leave the car, she's sure to be discovered.

Chapter 30

Weakening Signal

It's good to feel strong again, Victor Marius thinks as he climbs his makeshift radio tower for the fourth time in a single evening. During the days, he climbs up and down utility poles while supervising wire installations in Boston's Back Bay area. Then at night he continues to climb, trying to get his tower and his equipment ready for an important test.

But he realizes, during his fourth ascent, that only his body seems in shape. His mind, on the other hand, is increasingly unable to focus. The only reason he's climbing the tower again is that he forgot to bring his tools with him during his last climb.

He tightens some bolts and strings on a new wire. His heart isn't in it. Which seems strange to him, because he felt excited just a few minutes before. He curses himself for his fluctuating mood.

He wonders if his problems are related to his long work hours. He doesn't give himself a break because he's not happy about where he is right now. But he doesn't see any affordable way to leave the day job and focus solely on his radio experiments.

After another five minutes, he throws his wrench to the ground in disgust and climbs down, heading to bed.

I need to go see Professor Alton again, Victor thinks as he washes his hands and face. *Maybe he can help me run some more tests.* Then, before bed, he takes another shot of his special elixir. The relaxed feeing washes over him like a wave at first. Then the steroid kicks in later. Binging back the edge. The dread.

Victor lets out a long, grueling cough before settling down for the night. He needs to get more sleep. Yet it doesn't come.

The inspiration. That's what has kept him working all this time. Now, for some reason, the inspiration is starting to wane. Hopefully Professor Alton will be able to help him stoke that up again. He needs to find the same level of excitement that he felt just a few weeks ago when he bought this old brick building. That's the only way he's going to be able to continue pursuing his dream.

Unable to sleep, he gets up and injects a little more. As it takes its hold, he leans against a wall, slides down, and stares off into space.

Chapter 31

Absence

"God damn it!"

The words fill the hall and join the heavy footfalls Jeb Thomas creates as he charges up and down the third-floor hallway of the Great Bear Hotel.

"God damn her! She can't! She wouldn't!"

The men who have gathered at the hotel with Jeb are unable to console him. He kicks over her suitcase, which the ticket agent delivered to the room.

Grumbles and complaints about the noise drift out of the other hotel rooms.

The woman who manages the rooms appears, tying the tattered belt on her long bathrobe as a cigarette dangles from her mouth.

"You need to quiet down right now!" she scolds. "We have people sleeping here! They're paying customers!"

He tries to gain the manager's sympathy.

"She left me, Dolly. Amanda … she just up and left."

The woman gives a little snort. "Well, what did you think was going to happen, ya fool? This ain't no place for a woman. No one's going to come out here and wait forever for a man to conduct his business."

She waits for him to respond, but he only stares at the floor.

"Men come here and they settle in for weeks and months," she continues. "I know how it goes. Women tend to come and go even quicker." She sniffs a bit then takes a puff on her cigarette. "Truth be told, I've grown tired of having you around too."

She pushes at Jeb, turning him around in the hall and urging him back toward his room.

"What am I going to do?"

"Well," she whispers, "what do you want to do?"

"I don't know. I feel like I should go after her. Maybe apologize. But then … should I? I mean, she knew why we were here. She knew it would take time, and she seemed to sign on for that. Least I thought."

Dolly shrugs. "A woman walks out on you, it's never a good thing. Means she's given up on you. Seen things in you she didn't want to be there. Why would you want her back if she's lost that faith?"

Jeb sits on his bed and looks at his shoes.

Dolly lights a second lamp in the room and heads back to the door. Then she turns to look at him.

"How long were you together?"

"Just a few weeks," he mutters. "Seems like more though. A lot more."

"You had big plans?"

"Guess I did. Guess I thought she did too."

Dolly nods. "Maybe she did. Can't be easy for either of you to give something like that up."

He looks at her hopefully.

"You want her back, don't ya?"

It takes him a while to nod, but he does so.

"Well, if you really do want her, cowboy, go after her. Only a couple of ways out of this town. If she ain't got a horse, she has to take a train. You go down to the station. Maybe someone saw something."

"Yeah. Already had someone on the lookout there. She tried, but she didn't get on the train that night."

"Really? You mean someone tried to stop her?"

He shrugs.

Dolly exhales slowly. "Men!" She shakes her head then closes the door, with a stern warning that he has to keep his voice down for the rest of the night.

Early the next morning, Jeb stalks down the street toward the train station, a mix of anger, sorrow, and defiance on his face.

Something in Jeb snaps, and he grabs the ticket agent by his dark lapels when he finds him. "Where did she go? Why didn't you stop her?" he demands.

"Hey!" the man shouts. "You've got no cause to be angry with me. I did right by you, god damn it!"

Jeb slowly lets him go when others in the station turn to stare. "Sorry. Look, it's just …."

The agent indignantly smooths his jacket. "Besides, I did stop her. It's just like I told you when I brought you the suitcase. She didn't get on the last train out that night. I saw to that."

"You sure?"

"Quite sure. Conductor was with me on the plan. We watched both sides of the train. There's no way she's headed to Denver."

"All right. I'm sorry again, really." He smooths the man's coat, but his hand is pushed away. "Thanks for your trouble." He presses two dollars into the agent's hand.

Jeb returns to the hotel and sits on the front porch. He stares at the street for a while, trying to figure everything out. Is she still in town? Unlikely. She knows no one here. No good way for her to make a living, least not without a serious adjustment to her morality.

Did she catch a stage? Not a lot of stagecoach traffic anymore. Railway is a much better way to travel. But just to be sure, he walks to the stage office and asks a few questions. No, no one of Amanda's description has been in. Yes, they're sure. Only been one stage that left in the past two days, and it held three businessmen heading to Helena.

He also visits two local stables. No one rented a horse to a woman.

"If someone in town is missing a horse, would you hear about it?" he asks both stable managers.

Both boast that they would be among the first to know. "If someone is missing a horse," the second manager says, "first thing they do is ask around about it. The stables are the logical first places to ask. People try to sell horses to us all the time. You know, you might want to stop in and talk to the sheriff too. Maybe they can help ya." Jeb thanks him, but he knows it wouldn't be a good idea to show his face to any law enforcement officers right now.

Standing in the middle of Main Street, Jeb looks one way, then the other. He tries to place himself in her shoes. He tries to think of what she has in the way of traveling clothes, food, supplies. He slowly shakes his head.

"No," he mutters. Amanda didn't leave town by the road. She didn't take a horse, and she didn't catch a ride on some wagon. She wasn't set up for that. To make sure, he pays one last visit to the general store. He's right. She didn't come there looking for supplies or clothing. Any money she had was in her suitcase.

Hands thrust into his pockets, he heads back to the train station. The ticket agent sees him coming and eyes him with disdain. "I don't want no more trouble, you hear?"

Jeb holds up his hands in surrender. "No trouble. I promise. Just another question."

The agent looks exasperated.

"Is it possible that she got on that Denver train anyway? Without you seeing?"

"Look, anything is possible. But I don't think so. I really don't. When I caught her, she ran."

"Ran where?"

"Don't know. Into the woods first. Who knows from there?"

"And she didn't come back?"

"Not for that train. I watched for her."

"When did the next train come?"

"Not until morning. I 'spose she could have snuck aboard that one."

Jeb looks up the tracks. "No other trains come though during the night?"

"Well, sometimes trains that aren't scheduled to stop end up stopping here anyway. Older, smaller engines have to stop more often. They take on water. Some take coal. We got an honor system. They sign for what they take and we bill their company."

Jeb's eyes dart back and forth as he tries to absorb what this might mean. "And last night? Any trains?"

"I don't know. Might have been. I really don't pay much attention to them." He nods toward the water tower. There's a ledger hanging from a chain. He runs over and opens it. It lists just a train number, and a notation that they stopped to take on water the previous night.

Jeb looks at the ground. "Shit, shit, shit!"

"Well, if it's any consolation, she knew enough not to go that way." He points northwest. "So if she did get on that freight train, you know which way she went. Had to go southeast."

Jeb walks slowly away.

"What? No more tips this time for good information? You cheap bastard!"

But Jeb doesn't hear the words. He's trying to figure out what to do, and good ideas just aren't coming.

Chapter 32

Match

Mind in a haze, Victor wanders through Boston and finds himself alone this Friday night. His new friends, such as they are, have scattered for the weekend. Thurman took the train to Worcester for a wedding. Jimmy has a date, lucky lad. And Lucas? Well, Lucas was already drunk and asleep by six o'clock.

Victor feels especially edgy this evening. He gave himself two shots during the day. He's been shooting like that for several days now. Found that opium is easy to purchase in Boston's Chinatown. Meanwhile, the good doctor David Burke seems to have an endless supply of steroid compounds available for him to test.

So, after putting away his tools and finishing his bench-top experiments for the day, Victor takes a stroll toward the docks. The drugs make him feel both muted and satisfied. The opium feels euphoric. The steroid makes him focus on his newfound strength. Or maybe it's just endurance. In concert, the pair of drugs has created a vexing restlessness. It's a surreal combination, sparking an internal discourse that is simultaneously languid, and callous, and brutal. He's not sure what to make of it.

His clouded thoughts do not help. Nor does the fire in his muscles.

It's Friday night. Fight night. But now, there's no more Electric Kid to entertain and challenge the crowd. Silly as that whole episode was, fighting as the Kid gave him an outlet for his energy and his exasperation.

Victor knows he's grown enamored with the excitement and the carnival ambiance that can be found in that alley. So that's where he heads.

The noise can be heard from a block away. The crowd is heavier than usual. Word is out that John L. Sullivan is in the house. He's taking on challenges again, which always brings out a solid following and more noise.

Victor reaches the opening and quietly weaves his way through the narrow backstreet. He stops to watch a juggler. The man tosses whiskey bottles and takes a drink from an open one each time it passes. Then Victor stops to buy an apple, deep fried and sprinkled with cinnamon and sugar. The taste is a keen sensation. The smells are heavenly in some directions and rancid in others. Colors swirl.

Eventually he pays his dime and slides, along with the bulk of the crowd, into the warehouse. As usual, the inside air smells of sweat and cigar smoke. A hatch to the roof has been opened to help draw air across the ring. Young boys in flannel caps peer down through the hole.

A cheer goes up, but Victor is too far from the ring to see what happened. By the time he gets close enough, the topless ring girl (actually a rough-looking woman of 40) holds up a sign that simply says *Match #2*. Someone from the crowd pours beer over her breasts as she leaves the ring. At first, she looks angry, then she lets out a long "woo" and shakes it off like a golden retriever.

The second fight of the main card gets underway. It's two young boys, maybe 13 years old. Even in his foggy state, Victor is dismayed by this part of the event. Sometimes the managers of the fights need to fill out their program for the evening, but not enough real fighters are available. So, they'll recruit participants from a small Southie orphanage. He's heard the boys aren't always willing participants. Money is exchanged with the priests who run the brick building, and then the chosen kids are told that they will be fighting. There will be hell to pay if they say no. But there are nice rewards, like an extra dessert, if they say yes.

This fight looks particularly uneven. One of the lads is a head taller than the other. He pummels the younger boy, who already has a bloody nose. Instead of punching back, the smaller lad just holds his gloves up in front of his face and backs away from the blows.

It seems like half the crowd is wildly cheering and enjoying the sordid spectacle, while the other half begins to look guilty for being spectators at an obviously unfair fight. Boos are heard. Victor wants to say something, but his head is swimming and he's not sure that he can even talk. Instead, he goes to sit on some makeshift bleachers. Eventually the smaller lad is knocked down. The fight is called and the referee holds up the gloved hand of the winner. The other boy stands too. He fights back tears.

The next two bouts are standard matches. All are boxers, legitimate contenders in their weight divisions, trying to fight their way up the ranking ladders. Victor takes a deep breath, shakes his head a bit, and starts to feel more alert. He flexes instinctively. He's been doing that a lot lately, and it feels good. He's been hitting the weights heavily for the past week. He's also been shadowboxing at night when he can't sleep.

He even stands and cheers for one of the close and hard-fought matches.

Then the announcer, standing on a stool mid-ring while shouting into a megaphone, calls for a pause in the action. The final fight of the night, a championship middleweight match, will take place after the break. But much of the crowd quickly walks toward a side-ring that looks like no more than a roped-off square. Crates of various heights have been stacked around the outside, giving people more places to stand and watch.

This is the spot where the great John L. will take on all comers. Bare knuckles. One round each. Challengers pay to fight.

Victor buys a beer and slowly works his way to the front of the crowd. Instinctively he flexes his arm as he curls the beer up to his lips.

In his hazy state, it's like he can feel every sinew in every muscle. He feels both muted and strangely alive. Wickedly more than human.

Eyes wide, Victor watches one fight, then another. The room seems to swim again. He feels mesmerized by the scene unfolding. Sullivan hits hard and usually ends things quickly. But Victor notices the aging fighter growing a little more weary after each bout. After six challengers, the ringmaster calls out for more. "Come and challenge the Boston Strong Boy!" he implores. "Be part of the legend!"

Victor knows now exactly why he's wandered to this place. But will he actually step up? Should he? He already knows the answer.

Just climbing into that ring will be a victory for him. Tonight he will be stronger than he has ever been. Stronger than he was before the wreck of the Gossamer. Braver too. Tougher. He must do this. He needs to prove to himself and to others that he's back, and better than ever.

As another challenger steps forward and starts to fight the great man, Victor makes his way to the small folding table beside the ring. He puts down a few dollars, signs a paper, and takes off his shirt.

He stretches as he watches the other fighter take a few swipes at Sullivan. As he does so, he also sees a man in a suit, along with policemen, approach the table to chat with the man who's taking the money.

In the ring, Sullivan seems to toy with his opponent. He holds him at arm's length, waiting for the man to swing. The punches never quite land. Then Sullivan punches the gent hard in the stomach, and gives him a quick uppercut. The challenger falls onto his back, dazed. He slowly turns his head to the left and vomits.

Sullivan laughs and takes a stroll around the ring, arms raised, while the crowd cheers.

Victor steps through the ropes and into the square, then waits while a mop boy cleans the boards. Behind him, coming from the direction of the table, he can hear arguing.

Someone is quoting something about the law. But the referee signals the start. The bell rings. In his daze, it sounds like a fog horn to Victor.

Sullivan gives him a quick nod. Both men raise their bare fists and start to circle. The bulk of the crowd cheers for the famous fighter. But Victor does hear a few supporting voices. They call for him to "show that old man what you've got."

They move close, then back up. Sullivan is an expert at protecting his face and gut. Victor throws a few jabs, but they bounce off the big man's hands and forearms.

"You think you're a fighter, eh lad?" Sullivan demands. He swings a quick, hard right. It doesn't connect. Victor has learned how to dodge, but he can feel the breeze just an inch from his nose. He should be terrified by the near miss, but he just smirks.

The wide swing allows Victor to throw another jab before Sullivan can pull his arm back into place. It bounces off the boxer's shoulder. To Victor, it felt like a good solid hit. It would have sent most men stepping back a pace or two. But Sullivan barely notices the impact.

They parry some more.

"I saw you last week, lad," Sullivan says as they circle each other. "I was in the crowd. I saw you with your electric wires. What happened eh, lad? Lose your wires?"

"Had to give 'em up," Victor replies. "This place doesn't like the competition."

Sullivan smiles and tips his head toward the men at the table. "No, they don't. And neither do I." With that, he punches straight in, catching Victor under the left eye. It rocks him hard, and he feels the jolt right down to the base of his neck. But as Victor spins slightly with the impact, he instinctively brings around a right hook. The impact of his fist against Sullivan's ear is the only thing that keeps Victor from toppling over. But to the crowd, it looks and sounds like another good solid hit, and they cheer.

Sullivan steps back in surprise. Then laughs. "Ah, you do have some fight in you, I see." As they spin, punch, and parry, the older man laughs. "Only one of us is bleeding though, lad. You see that, don't ya? It ain't me."

Victor can feel the drops running down his cheek from a cut under his swollen eye. Unlike a regular match, no ref will stop an exhibition match because of a cut. It's up to each fighter to decide what to do.

Two policemen, along with one of the men from the table, approach the side of the ring. They motion to the referee.

Victor suddenly can feel the weight of his arms as he holds them up. Blocking each of Sullivan's rapid and hard punches takes its toll. The impact is transferred to all other muscles in his arms and shoulders. But even through his muted haze, he can sense that Sullivan is growing tired too. Keeping those massive arms high is a lot of work.

A punch that hits his face actually clears the cobwebs from Victor's head. Now, a rush of energy kicks in. He takes a new approach. He stands back a bit, just out of reach, and makes Sullivan take a step toward him. He does it again. And he makes sure he steps in such a way that Sullivan is forced to always take the step with his right foot, which leaves his left foot and arm back just a bit. Victor does this several times, waiting for just the right opening, and when he sees it, he takes his swing. That swing comes with a level of intensity and anger that Victor never knew he possessed.

It's like the punch gathered its momentum from somewhere far away. Somewhere out to sea. It's a heavy blow, collecting speed like a summer storm. Victor drives the fist in a great curve, like it's swinging down through Cape Cod, then up through the south shore. Past the beaches. Past rows of electrical wires. Past every hole and bump on the road. In his mind, he swings that fist up past the triple deckers of South Boston. Then on into this downtown waterfront, with great fury and determination, toward the face of a man Victor actually admires, but who has come to embody a giant that needs to be slain.

The fist hits hard with rage and resentment, driven home by months of hopes and dreams, failures and tragedies. The connection makes a resounding smack. Sullivan's head twists, jaw pressed askew. Beads of sweat fly like fireworks. He staggers back, turns and drops to one knee. Then both knees. The crowd cheers loudly. Then silence descends. The referee, who has done practically nothing so far, steps forward and holds up a finger, telling Victor to wait. Victor cocks his head and watches.

What he sees is like the back of a great bear, rising up with anger in its heart and murder in its fat paws. Sullivan stands tall, takes a breath, and turns back toward the center of the ring. The taunting but convivial showman is gone now. In its place is a freight train of anger.

And he comes back, arms punching like pistons. Victor holds up his fists, blocking blow after blow. The impact drives him inch by inch toward the ropes behind him. The exhibition part of the match stopped with Victor's hard, well-landed punch. Now, the risen Sullivan is suddenly all-professional in his stance and in his approach. But it's the anger behind the blows that's genuinely terrifying.

Victor dodges a fast hook, manages to land one more punch on the Boston Strong Boy's lip, then gets a punch to his own mouth in return. He sees a white light, but doesn't go down. Victor steps forward, swinging wildly, making contact with about half of the punches. But the fight is greeted with a flurry of whistles and shouts. The referee steps in to break them up. The two policemen step in behind him.

"What the hell!" Sullivan exclaims, holding up his hands in confusion.

Victor spits a little blood, then shouts, "You're not breaking this up! We're still…"

But the referee picks up his megaphone and talks to the crowd rather than the fighters. "That's it, folks. Sorry. Looks like bare knuckles gets shut down tonight by the commission. All done here."

The crowd boos. Some folks laugh. Curses are shouted toward the man in the suit, but the protests will have little effect. The law is the law. No more bare knuckles in Massachusetts. And since this whole warehouse fight business is sketchy legal ground, the managers aren't going to squawk too loudly about this inconvenience.

Sullivan walks to his corner and grabs a towel.

Victor hold up his heavy tired hands. "So that's it?"

"Looks like that's it, lad. Thanks for the bout. You're still alive. Be thankful."

"What the …"

But suddenly the crowd swarms into the ring. Several people slap Victor on the back or shake his hand. "By God you did it!" someone says. "You knocked the great John L. to his knees!"

Victor is stunned. "Yes, but… I mean, he got up."

"You know how many people he's fought here? Dozens. Maybe even a hundred. Not one challenger pulled off a punch like that. Not one! You staggered him!"

Someone puts his arm around Victor's shoulder and shouts in his ear. "Damn fine! Of course, he was ready to godamn kill you. Huh? Good thing the fight was called."

"Aw, never mind that!" an old man tells Victor. "You enjoy your moment, young man. That was one hell of a fight for an amateur."

As Victor enjoys his praise, he sees Sullivan shake his head and gather the rest of his things. He heads toward the door, stopping to sign an autograph along the way. Victor can see that the man is a true professional. He can turn his anger off and on as needed. Once the fight was called, all the steam was released from his freight train. It's like the old boxer went from blind rage to just another craftsman finishing up a night's work.

Someone hands Victor a cigar. Eventually the crowd moves away, off to the main bout.

Blood drips from his cheek. Also from his knuckles. Every muscle above his waist hurts. He takes a breath and looks around. He's still standing. He actually proved something to himself. Maybe to others too.

Occasionally someone catches his eye and gives him a thumbs-up.

Victor also gathers his things. Grunts a bit as he pulls on his shirt. The crowd is still thick in the area between the main ring and the exit. So thick, in fact, that Victor can't navigate through the throng. Instead, he doubles back and cuts beneath the bleachers. He can barely stand under the back row, but the gap provides a clear shot toward the front door. He's only about four feet into the cramped space when someone calls out from behind him.

"Hey," says the female voice. "Hey, you did all right back there."

He turns to see a woman of about thirty. She's very pretty, yet slightly rough-looking. Not a streetwalker, he supposes, but a woman who's used to being part of this sort of course crowd. Maybe a barmaid. Maybe a worker at one of the nearby factories. Carriage in good shape, but wear and tear on the wheels.

"Thank you." He smiles at her.

She follows him under the bleachers. Approaches him boldly. The tight space fills with her perfume. It's a quality scent, not a cheap one. Her clothes are old, probably secondhand. But they are fine linen and silk. Her blondish hair is clean and styled, but slightly tarty in the way it drapes across her forehead. She is a fascinating mix of exquisite taste, meager circumstances, and moral ambiguity.

"Still have some of that energy left?"

He looks puzzled. Starts to respond, but feels like his words and thoughts are stuck in some thick syrup. Tonight's punches to the head, combined with opium, make for a confusing and dream-like state.

But his response is not needed. She leans into him. Her hands roam. She feels his arms, his chest, his crotch, then pulls him in for a kiss. He can feel her hunger. Her heat.

Just as he came to fight tonight, she came to this building for exactly this. His name doesn't matter. He can tell that he's simply the prey she has settled on. His performance in the ring sealed the deal, and she came looking.

He thinks about resisting. But her touch is euphoric. It's been a long time since he's been with a woman. Too long. And this woman, for all her roughness and boldness, has a strange and seductive beauty.

His judgement peels away as fast as her blouse. She undoes his belt. They draw together.

It's not a romantic encounter, but it's a rough, animalistic, and intense one. His anger from the ring has not totally abated, and that seems to be exactly what she seeks.

Sweat and smoke seem to have penetrated the very wood of these bleachers. She kisses him, but action is more like an afterthought. They fall deeper into it with no qualms. The metal bleacher supports rattle, but the noise of the crowd hides the furor of their encounter.

It's over in a matter of minutes. They catch their collective breath and lean against each other. Silence and smiles. He again smells the perfume on her neck.

Then she kisses him, and is gone. It takes him a minute to get his bearings.

As he comes out from the far end of the bleachers, he feels a great weariness set in. So much wear-and-tear tonight. So much to think about. But actual real thinking, such as it is, will have to wait until tomorrow.

Ignoring the pulsing sound of the warehouse as it seems to swim past him, Victor walks out into the night. Behind him he can hear cheers as the main fight of the evening, a legitimate, sanctioned, and apparently highly anticipated bout, gets underway.

This part of the city still has gas streetlights. He finds a discarded piece of lath and holds it up to the flame. Then he lights his cigar.

At the end of the long pier, he leans against a piling and takes a deep puff. The tobacco is soothing. The only sound is shallow waves. A lighthouse shows itself from across the bay. Two flashes, a delay, then two more.

He's not sure how long he's been standing here, but the cigar is half gone when he hears footsteps, then someone stands beside him.

"That was a good punch, lad. Didn't think you had it in you."

He turns to see John L. Sullivan. He's changed into a suit and tie, and he now looks just as fit and prosperous as any of the men who were betting on their fight earlier in the evening. Victor laughs. "Too bad they broke it up, hum? We'll never know who might have won."

Sullivan chuckles. Then lights his own cigar.

"I usually don't fight men who are as intoxicated as you. And we both know you were. It's a fool's game. That kind of challenger either goes down quickly, or they keep swinging and they fight nearly to death. Either way, it doesn't look good for me."

"Intoxicated, hum?"

"You're certainly on something, lad. That much is clear. I looked into your eyes when we were in the ring, and all I saw was clouds."

Victor stares at the flashing beacon. "Yeah. I guess I was seeing clouds."

The two men stand in silence for a moment. It's Sullivan who finally speaks. "Well, you're certainly in great shape. I'll give you that. What you lack in skill you made up for in strength and enthusiasm."

Victor grins and says nothing.

"I don't know what your story is, lad. I know you had something to prove to yourself tonight, and I'd say you did it. But the fight game is a stupid way to make a living. I should know, eh? I don't care if you're wearing wires and batteries for show or just punching hard like a streetfighter. Either way will take a toll on ya. It's no life for a sane man."

"Ahh," Victor says with a nod. "There's the issue then. Sanity. That can be very tough to come by."

Sullivan just laughs.

They chat some more, until their cigars are burned down to stubs. Then Sullivan shakes Victor's hand. "Nice fighting with you, lad. And meeting you too. Just stay away from that damn alley, okay? I know you have something else going on. I can tell by the way you talk. I can tell by the way you act. You've got a brain in there. You don't need someone rattling that pan so that brain is no good anymore."

Victor shrugs.

"Boxing is for desperate men. Men who don't have much else to fall back on. That's where I was. Still am. Any one of the fighters I know, if we had something better to go to, we sure as hell wouldn't be taking punches. And we wouldn't be drowning our brains in whatever booze or drugs you've been using either."

He gives Victor a sly nod. "You think about that, smart guy."

And with that, walks away.

Victor takes a couple more puffs then flicks the cigar butt into the water. As he walks away from the pier and the warehouses, he's overcome with the weight of the day. He makes it for a few blocks, toward the Public Garden, but soon realizes he doesn't have the energy to walk all the way home. Instead, he slips into the doorway of a building, slides down the wall, and passes out in a bruised and ragged heap.

Chapter 33

Second Entry

Devlin remembers the route. Low-hanging wooden drainpipe at the end of a group of row houses. Climbing up, he can get to the top of a first-floor kitchen. From there, he can grab another drainpipe, this one copper, to hoist himself up to the rooftops. In the dark, the climb takes less than a minute.

A dog barks inside one of the houses, but no one comes to the windows. He's up on the roof, making his way toward the Morgans' house with very little trouble.

When he gets there, he peers through the window and sees no evidence of activity. The window is locked, but that shouldn't be much trouble. He pulls a simple flat kitchen knife from his pocket and slides it between the double windows. With a little vibration, he's able to lift the latch and step inside.

But the latch is not tightly attached, and as the door swings open, a small metal part drops loose and falls to the floor. The noise is minimal, but troubling. He decides to search the room quickly, in case the noise has given him away.

Downstairs Jonathan Morgan looks up from his paper. He squints toward the staircase then rises, walking to the base of the walnut bannister.

"Beverly?" he calls upward. There's no response. He realizes that Beverly is working in the kitchen.

He walks to a hall table and pulls open the top drawer. He removes something before proceeding to the stairs. Slipping off his shoes, he carefully climbs upward, step by slow step, trying to keep each board from squeaking. He does hear other boards squeaking softly though. Those boards are upstairs. Someone definitely is there.

On the third floor, Devlin works quickly. He lights a candle. Searches under the bed, in the closet, and in the room's small dresser. Getting bolder, he steps out in the hallway, listening. Then he checks a small closet that's near the top of the steps. Inside he finds only linens, but he pokes through each pile, just to make sure nothing's hidden beneath.

"I might have known you'd come back," a voice calls out from behind him. The thick wool of the carpet must have helped mask the man's footsteps.

Devlin spins toward the voice, hand sliding into his coat.

"No, no," Jonathan warns. He points a polished revolver directly at Devlin's chest. "I have every right to drop you right where you stand. I suggest you keep those hands where I can see them."

Devlin shoots him a nasty look but removes his hand from the pocket—without his weapon.

"Who are you?" Jonathan demands.

Devlin says nothing, but not just because he doesn't want to offer any clues. This man, this proper Yankee gentleman, reminds him of all the reasons he hates the North. He decides this is a good time to keep his southern heritage hidden, and that means not opening his mouth to ask a question.

"You're here for that damn box, aren't you?"

Devlin shrugs.

"Did you really think that I'd be stupid enough to keep it in the house again?" His voice rises in anger. He thrusts the gun in front of him as he speaks.

"You're the one who came before, aren't you? Do you know how much trouble you brought into the house? Do you even know what you ended up chasing away from here?"

Devlin starts to feel worried. This so-called gentleman just might be angry enough to shoot.

"Jonathan? Is that you?" Beverly calls from below. "What are you doing? Who are you talking to?"

"Stay down there, Beverly!" Jonathan calls over his shoulder.

That's all the distraction Devlin needs. He dives at the floor, tucking tight and somersaulting forward. He's below where Jonathan has the gun trained, even as the old man tries to move it downward. This allows Devlin to kick hard as he comes out of his roll. The blow catches the old man at his knees and sends him teetering, then falling backward down the stairs.

For a moment, Devlin considers charging down the steps and grabbing the gun. He hears Jonathan moaning and struggling to stand up. Devlin looks, sees that he still grasps his gun, and decides to run instead. He sprints back into the bedroom and literally dives out the open window. Sliding onto the tin shingles.

Jonathan does manage to stand. His back is tremendously bruised from the fall, and he has blood trickling from a gash on his head. But he steels himself, grabs the railing, and climbs back up toward the attic.

"Come back here!" he shouts. "Come back here right now, you bastard!"

"Jonathan?" Beverly calls from below. Ignoring his warning to stay put, she too starts climbing up the stairs.

Following the criminal out onto the roof, the silver-haired man spies the other man climbing over the roof next door. Moonlight shines off his gray coat. Jonathan fires twice. The shadow slips down the far side.

"Jonathan, what on earth?" Beverly cries as she leans out the window.

"He came back," Jonathan said. "Our intruder came back. I caught him in the hallway. Has to be the same man."

"And you tried to stop him? And you tried to shoot him?"

"I did, indeed."

"Jonathan! You might have been killed!"

"Bah, stop yelling at me, woman. A man has a right to protect his own home."

She sees the direction that Jonathan is looking, and she looks there too. "Did you get him?"

Jonathan shakes his head and places the gun in his pocket. "I don't think so. But he knows we mean business. He won't be coming back here tonight. Hopefully not ever."

Pulling out a handkerchief, he dabs at the blood that's now running onto his shoulder. "I need to get this stitched up. Then we need to fill out another police report. I'm getting tired of this, I can tell you that much."

Beverly looks close to tears. "I used to think this was such a nice, safe neighborhood. What's happened, dear? Do you think we need to move?"

Chapter 34

The Bottom

Victor comes awake at the first light of dawn. He looks out from his doorway. At least it looks like a doorway. Where the hell did he sleep? He sees a rat heading down the street. It turns left and disappears down an alley.

He stumbles to his feet. His body screams in protest. He has not woken up this sore and spent since he was thrown from a horse at age eight. He wipes dried blood from his face and stumbles down the sidewalk. He should go home to get some sleep. He should get something to eat. He should do… something. But more than anything else, what he really wants to do is put that needle in his arm again.

This is not where he ever expected to be.

Teeth grinding, he walks across the Public Garden and toward the Charles River. He pulls the syringe, the opium, and the steroid bottle from his pocket. He thinks about how good it will feel to inject the mix again. He things about how quickly it will erase the pain he's feeling. It will also erase the need for him to do anything today. Anything at all.

As he approaches the river, he can see a group of men in the distance. They all wear white shorts and athletic shirts, and they are jogging toward him on a dirt path that runs beside the river. Victor ignores them. Instead, he walks to the river bank, staring deeply into the current. In his present state, he realizes he must look like a bum or a beggar.

He looks at the bottle and the needle in his hand. Looks at the water. Looks back again. Then he raises his arm and flings the whole lot into the water.

One of the joggers notices the needle and vials and slows to a stop. He calls to the other men, telling them he will catch up.

Victor gives him a curious look.

"That's a good thing that you did there," the jogger says.

"What do you mean? How do you even know what I did?"

"I saw the syringe. I recognized those vials. I'm a medical student. At Harvard."

Victor nods. His head hurts.

"Most people smoke opium. But I know you can inject it too. I know because I tried it. It feels good. Takes your worries away. For a while anyway."

"Yeah. For a while." Victor closes his eyes and takes a deep breath.

"Look, that's a nice coat you have there. Or at least it used to be. But it's all dirty now. Blood stains too. You look like shit. I think you know that."

Victor nods. "Been feeling like shit too."

"It's a bad thing. I stopped because I recognize you."

"You do?"

"That's… okay, that's not exactly what I meant. I guess I recognized myself. You look a lot like I did eight months ago. In medical settings, I had easy access to morphine. Same shit. More concentrated probably. I tried some. Then tried some more. Then my world shrank down."

Victor nods. He feels slightly queasy, and knows he needs another dose. But it's gone now, just like he wanted it to be.

"How did you stay away?" Victor asks him. "You know how it makes you want it. It's so tough to walk away."

"I guess I didn't walk away. I ran. That's how I kicked it. Running with this club became my new drug. The temple of the body, when the body is in shape, helps sculpt the sanctuary of the mind."

He turns to look toward his friends. He needs to catch up. But before he does…

"Listen. I'm Anthony. Tony, okay? And you are…?"

"Victor." They shake hands. The grip is earnest.

"Listen, Victor. We run here each day. Three to five miles. Join us if you want. The other guys know my story. They'll be accepting of you too."

"Maybe. I'd like to. But not sure I'll be in very good shape tomorrow."

"Day after then. And you don't have to do the whole distance."

Victor nods. "I might join you. We'll see. Thanks for the invite, Tony."

Tony takes off at a fast clip up the path as Victor turns back toward home. He knows his energy will be spent on recovery for the next day or two. But he still finds the vitality to put a little spring in his step.

Chapter 35

A New Design

"I think I understand where you went wrong. You actually have too much power, not too little, and it needs to be channeled into the coil a different way. See attached sketch for an idea on alternative wire placement."

Victor reads a letter with the words from his friend Nikola. A smile slowly forms on his face. *Yes, of course. He's quite correct*, Victor thinks. *I've been forcing far too much current into the coil to get the results I wanted.* No wonder sparks were flying and things were burning. They were going down the wrong path. Victor studies Tesla's notes and schematics for several minutes.

It was tough for him, these past few days. His body reacted violently to the lack of drugs. Muscle aches. Vomiting. Cramping and sweats. But Victor is feeling better now. Much more solid, grounded and sober. He gets back to work.

It all makes sense now. Every coil he ever built, right down to the one he carried with him on the ship, contained the same basic flaw. Too much current and it could arc out into the air. In retrospect, he's lucky he didn't electrocute himself or someone else!

Victor walks to his workbench and pulls out his latest coil. Looking at Tesla's design, he removes some wires then inserts a capacitor based on a simple Leyden jar design. He then reverses the polarity and reduces the total power going into the coil.

Smiling, he steps back to test it again. But when he throws the switch, nothing happens.

Turning the power off, Victor checks all his work again, and checks the notes too. He does some more tests but still gets no spark at all. Running his fingers through his hair, he tries to think. Grabbing Tesla's drawings, he reviews them again, but this time he calls upon every memory he has. Something still is wrong. It's something minor, and only a hard-core engineer can pick up on it. But he feels that he's up to the task.

He makes a cup of coffee and sits outside, reviewing the papers.

The problem, he decides, is in the capacitor design. He also notes a few complicating factors related to Tesla's drawing. A small coil and some taped wires should fix it. After making the changes, he tries again. The coil hums to life. In a few seconds, he hears the familiar tick of the spark.

When he checks his receiver, Victor sees, by far, the strongest signal he's ever received. Tesla's idea had the basics correct. Extra power was not the answer. Different arrangement of the current flow was the answer. And it was Victor's final idea that made the whole thing work.

With this significant success under his belt, Victor immediately turns his attention toward building a new longer-range transmitter.

His first thought is just to build a larger, more powerful version. But within two hours, he realizes that he needs to totally rethink his approach.

On a whim, he makes yet another modification to the capacitor, and adds two more. Then he sets up a group of circuits rather than a single circuit, and starts to build a set of parallel transmitters that will operate at the same frequency. It's one of several approaches he intends to try over the next few days.

It's late at night by the time Victor retires. He falls into bed, but wants to reread the letter from Tesla before he falls asleep.

The drawings hold no new clues for him. But he does take another look at the last few paragraphs of the letter. In these, Tesla returns to his rant about being able to broadcast images and messages and even electricity around the globe. Victor isn't sure whether to feel a sense of excitement from Tesla's ideas, or to worry about him. The very idea that one can broadcast electricity pretty much defies the laws of physics as scientists understand it, so his mentor is either a genius or a madman. Victor isn't sure he wants to draw a conclusion either way right now.

He turns off the electric light that dangles over his bed, locks his fingers under his head, and stares into the darkness.

But it's not quite dark. The wire inside the light bulb above him still retains a slight glow. He finds himself staring at it, wondering how long it will be before that glow fades.

When it finally does, he reaches up, flicks the light on once again, and then flicks it off. The glow is back, again slowly fading, but still quite noticeable.

Like me? he thinks.

Having come so close to death, the strangest thing to Victor is that life is so fragile, and so impossible to restart once it has stopped.

What is it, exactly, that makes his life ... well, a *life*? How is it different from something that is lacking life?

When working with wires, the physics of the process is simple. Plug a wire in, and it becomes "live." A completed circuit has power flowing through it. Then, if you unplug the circuit, everything stops. The power and the energy that was there—it's suddenly gone. The circuit is dead.

The difference is, if you plug the wires back in again, viola! The power returns.

So why doesn't life force work that way too? You can't stop a life and then put it back. If someone dies, it's the same as if they've been unplugged. But you can't plug them in again. All the elements may be there. The same body. The same brain the same eyes. But the sustaining power of life can't be brought back once it's been cut.

And there's something even stranger. Not only can't you restore a life once it has been ended, you can never really create it in the first place. Much as parents like to pat themselves on the back for creating a new life, the life doesn't come *from* them. It comes *through* them.

Victor doesn't like to use the word "God" as a way of explaining anything. "God" is a human word used to attempt to define something that is far beyond our comprehension. The very act of trying to define it actually trivializes the concept, in his mind. Though he can't find fault with those who find some level of solace in organized religion.

He flips the light switch again. On. Off. The glow returns, and fades.

Yes, indeed. What exactly *is* life? And what exactly is this thing that exists in the mind of the living? And Tesla's ideas, do they mark some new, highly evolved thought process? Will the world soon be racing to catch up? Or do Tesla's ideas represent something different? Perhaps the decay of a once-great mind that has become overtaxed by its own genius?

Victor watches the light bulb's glow fade to black.

He doesn't have the answers. All he has is lingering doubts—even over the state of his own mind, and his own affairs.

What he needs, he thinks while drifting off to sleep, is just the proper inspiration for keeping his mind on track. He's onto something big now. He may very well have found the proper method for sending a long-distance radio signal. What he doesn't want to do is end up like Tesla, with so many big, glorious ideas that he can't even make them a reality.

The next morning, he gets up very early, and waits near the start of the dirt path by the river. He wonders if his drugs are still at the bottom of the Charles River, or if they have been swept downstream. Eventually the group of runners, dressed in their usual white, comes jogging toward him. Tony slows when he sees Victor, and jogs in place, then nods. Victor joins them, and they run on into the foggy morning. Up the river toward the east side of Boston. Toward the rising sun.

Chapter 36

Forsaken

A man with a brown coat and denim hat tugs at the cow nearest the door. He grows angry when the animal chooses not to budge toward a makeshift ramp. He starts tugging harder, placing a foot against the cow's stanchion stall.

"Roy? What you doing there, Roy?" someone shouts from outside the car.

"You never mind what I'm doing. You just tend to your flags and leave me be, ya hear?"

"Well, what *are* you doing? Why you taking a cow off the train? That ain't right. They's got rules about touching the cargo!"

The man pulling at the cow waves him away. "You don't be telling anyone about this, ya hear? This one's mine to take."

"What are you saying, Roy? The hell it's your'n. Doesn't matter if we're just caboose men. Both of us got some responsibility for the cargo. You know what? I'm going to get Ernest! Right now. I'm telling him."

Amanda draws her knees up against her chest, making herself as small as possible. She continues to listen.

"Listen, you damn fool," Roy replies. "You just hold on. Look, we've got us an interesting situation here, and I guess I can let you in on it. Somehow, we got us an extra cow on the train, okay? We was supposed to take on nine. But the fool back at the yard let ten wander in. I seen it. I didn't say nothing. Now, you go ahead and count 'em. How many you see?"

From her hiding place, Amanda sees a second head poke into the car. It bobs up and down.

"Eight, nine... ten. Well, I'll be damned. You're right!"

"I know I'm right. I counted 'em as they was loaded. And I counted them again right after he left. Ten head of cattle. Ain't that something? So what do you think? Who should benefit from this mistake? The guy who's buying the lot of 'em? Or me?"

The flagman thinks about this for a moment. "Well, I see where this is headed. Yes, sir. But I'd say us, not just you. Honest mistake and we're the ones who caught it. I can say that much, yes, sir."

Amanda closes her eyes, already tired of this man's sprawling gibberish.

"What do you mean 'us'? I'm the one who caught the mistake, damn it."

"So what? We both here. Right? You and me? Yes, sir. Yes, sir. Fifty-fifty split. That's what I say."

The cow thief shakes his head. "You ain't even supposed to be on this train! We didn't need a flagman! You're just hitching a ride." Roy rubs his chin. "I'll go seventy-thirty and not a penny more, ya fool. Finder's got a right to have an advantage. Besides, I'm the one who's got to find a buyer once we get this damn thing offloaded."

"All right. Fine. Fine and dandy then. But what are you going to do with it? Huh, Roy? Can't sell it out here, Roy! No, sir. Ain't no one around here for miles and miles!"

"I'm taking her down. See those planks there? We got us a shitty but workable ramp."

"Taking her down for what? Come on, Roy, what fer? You just going to leave her?"

Roy shakes his head, losing patience. "Damn it! I'm moving her back to the car sitting in front of our caboose. There's room there. It's practically empty. We can bring it in the side door. I just need to keep this cow out of sight when the other ones get dropped off late tonight."

"The dickens you say. You're going go ahead an' do that, Roy?"

"Well, why the hell not? This train gets split off when we get to Cheyenne. Back end of the train, us in the caboose, we're headed to Chicago. What better place to sell a cow than in Chicago, eh?"

"How much them cows go fer?"

"If it's a good day, I might get twenty-eight dollars."

"No kidding. That would be, what, seven or eight dollars to me? Well, hell, yeah, I'm in. Let's go!"

With that, the other man tests the boards and climbs up into the cattle car to help tug. The cow moves to the door but has no interest in stepping onto the steep ramp. The pushing and pulling doesn't work. Finally, the one called Roy picks up a board and starts whacking the beast on the back. After four blows, the cow lets out a sad bellow. But it doesn't move, and Roy resumes whacking.

Amanda places the knuckle of her index finger between her teeth and bites down hard.

"I said move, you beast. Move now! We got a schedule to keep!"

"Get that other board over by the front. See it?"

"Huh?"

"Over there, damn it!" Roy points. "That one's got a nail in it, see? Pick it up and poke her with the nail. It'll move to get away from that, I'll bet."

The flagman picks up the board and starts poking. The cow moos in anger, but steps slowly onto the ramp. Its feet start to slide. In a panic, it tries to back up. But its retreat is greeted with more pokes with the nail. The animal is in a panic now, sliding, stepping, and howling in pain.

Amanda keeps silent and curses herself for doing so. But she reasons that, even if she tries to stop them, they'll still force the animal off the train anyway, and they're likely to be just as mean and nasty to her once she is discovered.

Suddenly she sees blood coming from the cow's back, and both the men are using the boards to hit the beast repeatedly. The cow starts to fall.

"Stop it!" she hears herself shout. "Stop hitting that poor animal, you stupid bastards!" It's like the words are coming from some other Amanda. It's the angry Amanda who goes too far sometimes, and who becomes dangerously tough.

This other Amanda shouts and takes her stand and becomes … what? Maybe what Amanda really is?

But as she stands to confront the men, she feels like this other, confrontational Amanda is just floating somewhere far away, not here in the middle of a cow car. It's like she's standing on a hill, looking down on herself, feeling righteous and not caring about what happens to anyone else besides the silly cow.

Both men jump when she surprises them. The flagman falls backwards, like he's just seen a ghost. The caboose man swallows hard, but regains his composure quickly. He turns toward Amanda, brandishing the stick he was just using on the cow.

"Who the hell are you?"

Silence.

"What the hell? What are you doing in here? You come out of there right now. Out where we can see ya!"

The flagman stands back up and peers over the other cows. "Careful, Roy, she may have a gun. You got a gun, lady? She might have a gun, Roy. I'm telling you, she—"

"Shut up, you fool."

Amanda just stares at them.

The train shakes slightly. The locomotive crew has finished taking on water. The hatches have been closed, and the boiler is re-pressurizing.

"I said you come out of there, lady. We're authorized to drag you out if we find anyone stowing away. I don't think you should give us any trouble. Wouldn't be smart."

Amanda stands slowly and walks toward the door. She holds Roy's gaze, unrepentant.

"I was being chased. I had to get away. Your train was nearby, and it was an easy place for me to hide."

"Chased by who, lady?"

She wonders if it's wise to say. Do all railroad men know the same people? Will her story give her away?

"Someone who wanted me to stay in Butte. A man."

"She's a runaway, Roy. That's for sure. Ain't that a laugh, Roy? Looky that."

"I said shut up, you old dupe." He turns to Amanda and sneers. "That's a mighty fine story. But why'd you end up here? Huh? Why not go to the police?"

Roy looks her up and down. Amanda's clothes might have been nice twenty-four hours ago. But after hiding in the woods and climbing through a dirty cattle car, they look terrible and so does she. Self-conscious, hair askew, she tries to brush away some of the dirt on her dress.

"Yeah, what I see is a poor beggar woman who's just trying to steal a ride. Making up stories to cover that. Well, you know what? I might'a had some sympathy before. But not since you stopped me from getting my due by taking that there cow. And I sure as hell don't have any sympathy for someone who calls me stupid."

Amanda continues to look him straight in the eye. "Surely you realize …."

"Get out of this car now. You just git!"

She walks toward the door. "Where are we going?"

"'We' ain't going anywhere. Ned and me is going to Cheyenne. Then on to Chicago. But you, pretty lady, you can go to hell for all I care."

She steps down onto the ground. For the first time, she feels a sense of dread. "You're not going to just leave me out here!"

"Oh no? And what do you think you can do to stop us? That's what we're allowed to do with unauthorized riders, lady. Just set them out. That's the law. You stole the ride; you've earned the treatment. You're just lucky we're on company time. I might'a been a lot harder on ya if we wasn't. Might have had some good old fun if I wasn't in a hurry."

They argue for several minutes. Amanda lists her reasons for wanting to stay on the train. But Roy is seething with anger while his associate, Ned, just looks on, vapidly amused. Finally, a hundred yards ahead of them, the engineer tugs on the whistle, telling all that it's time to leave.

By this time, they've dragged the cow down the ramp, and they're walking it to the other car. Ned runs ahead with the boards, looking to make a new ramp up into the car. They ignore her and her pleas as she runs beside them.

Amanda feels a sense of panic setting in. This isn't what she anticipated. This can't be happening. There's nothing around here for miles.

"Please!" she says, throwing her hands up in despair. "You don't know what it's been like! You don't know what's happened to me!"

She tugs at Roy's coat, but he pushes her away. They manage to get the cow on board, and he slides the door shut. The two men walk back toward the caboose, continuing to ignore her.

"Please!" she shouts, following them down the track, past the other cars. "I have no money. I don't know anyone here. I have nowhere to go!"

The men walk back onto the caboose and shut the door. Amanda stands alongside, talking toward the windows. It's the first time she notices the dark clouds in the sky.

"Please! You can't do this! I don't even know where I am!"

Roy leans out the window. "You're in northern Wyoming. Best I can do for ya, girlie." He holds out a handkerchief and signals to the locomotive. With a chug and a hiss, the train starts to move.

In desperation she tries to run toward the locomotive. Maybe the engineer or the fireman will help her. But it's a losing battle. It's too far and the train just keeps picking up speed.

"Please! Just tell me!" she shouts as the caboose first pulls alongside her, then past. "Where can I go?"

"Don't know. Don't care. Just don't try getting back on the train. I'll kill ya if you do."

Ned leans out the other window, offering a mock tone level of sympathy. "Next town's a good seventy miles down the tracks from here! If I were you, lady, I'd keep walking. Don't try to follow the tracks though. Indians like to follow them too. Might have a good deal of fun with ya, if they catch ya! You just think about that!" He laughs a wicked little laugh, then salutes.

Amanda stops running and watches the train steam away.

At first, she's determined not to let this incident stop her. After all, nothing else has stopped her so far.

But as she turns away, looking at the landscape, her heart sinks. Her lower lip quivers. She's in Wyoming's high plains, the wide flat area between mountain ranges near the center of the state. This is not good news. It's wide and empty and desolate as a desert. She runs several hundred feet in one direction, up a very slight knoll that stands just a few feet higher than the surrounding ground. As far as she can see, the landscape barely changes. There's scrub grass and occasional short trees in one direction, but nary a house or a barn or even a thick forest for protection. She chooses another direction and runs to another slight knoll. Again all she sees is wilderness and flatness and mountains in the distance. Not even a line of wires on wooden poles. Not even a gathering of birds. Nothing.

Worried now, she runs in another direction, then another, 100 feet, 1,000 feet. It doesn't matter. There is nothing, anywhere, that draws her forward or gives her any sense that she's found a good direction. She's as lost as a person can be.

And then it starts to rain.

Amanda has never felt so alone. There's nothing here. No one. And no protection.

For some reason, her mind drifts back to that telescope in Boston. The one she looked through on the Fourth of July. She saw the mountains and plains of the moon. So empty and foreign. So peaceful. So far away.

Somehow, it's as if she's been transported to that empty place, and left there.

Amanda walks back to the tracks and falls to her knees. She finally lets herself cry. The emotion makes her feel weak and childish, but she can't stop it. It builds from a light sob to a full-scale flood of anguish, and it pours out of her like a lonely fury, mixing with the rain.

Eventually she slumps forward, head resting on the cool steel rail of the tracks. There will be no avenging angel sent to rescue her. Wet hair clings to the side of her face. She's so tired now. So very tired. Couldn't those stupid men see that? The fatigue and hopelessness start crushing her from the inside.

She thinks of everything, and she admits everything. The pain of the last few months, the long slow decline in the way she lives. The heartache of failure. She acknowledges her descent. She was a moral church-going woman, and now she's a tramp who rides the rails and commits adultery at will. She cries for lost friends and lost lovers. She cries for her life as a wife and a mother that never came to be. Her long cry is not so much for this day's failures, but for knowing, so intimately, day in and day out, what failure really is.

Hopeless. Penniless.

Wet. Cold.

Lost. So very lost.

So, there she stays. Forehead on the rail. Rain falling softly on her back. With no clear direction to go. The only reason to move would be to find a river. Maybe to drown herself.

Somewhere in the back of her mind, she remembers a song. It's a verse from something she heard in an old minstrel show that she saw years before. It was about a woman named Irene.

The words seem appropriate to her current situation. So she starts to sing it softly to herself, rocking back and forth and trying to forget her fears. She remembers only one stanza. Her soprano voice is thick with tears. Vulnerable yet lovely, it rolls over the plains like a tiny prayer.

Sometimes I live in the country.
Sometimes I live in the town.
Sometimes I get a great notion,
To jump in the river and drown.

She sings it over and over, lingering in her helplessness. But there is no river in sight. Even the simple escape of drowning, for now, is closed to her. It might be easier just to stay right here, head on the track, waiting for the next train.

End of Book 4

The Puzzle Box Chronicles is a series, starting with
Book 1
Wreck of the Gossamer

* * *

*

The Story of Amanda, Jeb, Wayne, Victor, Devlin and
others continues in

The Lost, the Found and the Hidden
The Puzzle Box Chronicles: Book 2

Those Who Wander
The Puzzle Box Chronicles: Book 3

Wires and Wings
The Puzzle Box Chronicles: Book 4

North of Angel Falls
The Puzzle Box Chronicles: Book 5

Deep in a Box of Waves
The Puzzle Box Chronicles: Book 6

Made in United States
Troutdale, OR
08/28/2023

12447053R00146